REPORTER SEEKS MOUNTAIN MAN

BEAR MOUNTAIN BROTHERS, BOOK 2

MARLEY MICHAELS

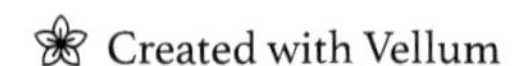
Created with Vellum

1

FAITH

"Oh my god, I can't believe you're finally here!" my best friend, Serena, cries, wrapping me up in a huge hug as soon as I step out of my beloved car, Bertha. She's definitely seen better days externally, but on the inside she's as good as they get. The old girl didn't let me down as we scaled the mountain.

Serena pulls back a little, and I hold her at arm's length. "There's no way I was missing out on being your Maid of Honor," I say, grinning like mad.

Serena beams with happiness. Like that shit is near pouring out of her. I love it. I love that she's found someone to make her smile like this. "Well, you're my best friend. And we promised each other when we were ten that we'd be each other's bridesmaids."

"We also promised we'd marry brothers so we'd be sisters," I say. "But I don't see myself settling down anytime soon. Not with the kind of deadlines they have me on at work." She follows me to the trunk where I pull out my bag.

"Wait...why do you only have a weekender?" she asks, closing the lid for me.

Damn. I was hoping to delay telling her my *slight* change of plans.

"Ummmmm...." I say, looking around the beautiful setup at the Bear Mountain Homestead. Serena gently grabs my arm, stopping me in my tracks. "Faith Marie Johnson. Tell me they didn't cancel your leave..."

"Ummmmm..."

"That's it. You *have* to leave that damn paper. This is just insane. That awful buttmunch needs to get a life so he'll stop disrupting yours." Buttmunch is the hilarious name Serena and I came up with to call my boss and editor, Marvin Markle. He's hated me since my Journalism Professor called in a favor with Giles Harris, the owner of the Anchorage Press newspaper, and voila, I was the new intern—*paid* intern. He'd wanted some desperate kid willing to work for nothing, but being told to hire me put an end to his expensive lunches charged to the paper, and he's had it in for me ever since. That was nine long months ago. Since then, two new interns have started and *both* get their pick of cool stories while I get thrown the work no one else wants to do and it sucks. Buttmunch is such a buttmunch.

"It's not that bad. I can stay till Monday. Then—"

"Ugh. This is *so* unfair. You work yourself to the bone for that paper and they treat you like you're an intern."

"I kind of *am* the intern, Reens."

"Well, yeah. But this is your best. friend's. wedding. We've had this booked for *two* months. You were *supposed* to be here for a *week*. I had all these plans to show you around the district and take you to meet Aster and—"

"Aster Hollingsworth?" I gasp.

"*Yes!* And you could've visited Kenshaw which is the town you drove through at the bottom of the mountain, and then there's a book club next week in Woodward Valley which is next to Moose Mountain. I was hoping to make you fall in love with the place so you'd wanna stay and never leave and then I'd have my best friend, my dad, *and* my husband, all living close again." Finished with her little tirade, Serena throws her hands in the air. "Ugh."

A quick glance toward the big building in front of me with a sign saying, 'The Den' shows her reaction has grabbed the attention of other homesteaders...*or are they residents?* I've never delved into exactly *how* this community works. But I'm fascinated by the concept. Everything Serena has told me about it makes it sound so magical and close-knit, but also with a real family-type feel.

"Sweet Pea..." Serena's soon-to-be husband, Brady Long, says softly, coming up behind her, giving me a chin lift. "Hey, Faith."

"Hey, Braaaadyyyy," I say. Even I swoon a little at how cute my best friend and her fiance are together. They look *amazing* for one. And two, I love that Serena is finally living the fairytale she always wished for but was always too busy helping out everyone else to get.

His grin turns into a sexier smirk as he turns his focus on his woman. "What did the doctor say about not getting too stressed?"

"I know," she says, stamping her foot. "But that stupid newspaper and that dumbass boss of hers! He...he...he's just a *fucker!*."

My eyes are bugging out at her outburst, but Brady just chuckles and shakes his head. "I'm starting to think I'm a bad influence on your good girl persona, sweet pea."

Serena looks up at him and I watch as all the tension in her body vanishes under his gaze.

"Wait...doctor? Stress?"

Brady pulls Serena into his side and she melts into him. "Your best friend was burning the wick at both ends with study and helping with the crops on top of planning our wedding. She fainted yesterday because she forgot to eat."

I narrow my eyes at my now-guilty bestie. "Serena Black, soon-to-be Long, don't make me tie you to the bed so you'll rest."

She gasps and I see that flash of fire in her gaze that I love goading out of her. "You *wouldn't.*"

I shrug. "Probably not. But he would." I point to Brady, who grins wickedly down at her before lowering his mouth to her ear and whispering something that makes her cheeks go red.

"And *that's* my cue to leave," I say, grabbing my suitcase handle and walking down the path before stopping and turning back around. "Um...where *exactly* am I going?"

"We have a guest cabin. I had the guys get it ready for you." Brady looks around before bringing his fingers to his lips and lets out a high-pitched whistle, which I swear goes on for a good ten seconds. It's like an orchestral arrangement with harmonies and everything.

A minute later a line of men emerge from behind The Den and I almost melt to the ground at the sight of them. No wonder Serena hooked herself to a mountain man. The group of men walking toward me could easily pass as cover models for Mountain Man

Monthly or something. Note to self, google whether there is actually a mountain man magazine in publication because if there is, I've got a 'man of the month' feature to pitch to them. If there's not, maybe I need to start one...

"Where's Walker?" Brady asks when the men reach us.

"He walked off muttering something about waste management and compost when we finished with the cabin. So I guess he's still working," one of them replies, before holding his hand out to me. "Nash. You must be Faith."

"Yeah. How'd you know?"

"Because Rena here has been buzzing about her best friend coming to visit for over a week now. She's been telling all the homestead about you."

"I have not...*much*..." Serena says, blushing a little.

"Aww, bestie. You love me."

She rolls her eyes. "Well, duh. Now let me introduce *most* of the mountain's founding sons." She points to Nash. "That's Nash. And from left to right, Micah, Tate, Miller, and Mason—"

"Let me guess," I gesture to Miller and Mason. "Twins?"

"Nah. We just look alike," Miller says, winking at me, earning groans from everyone and a giggle from Serena.

"And then there's Huxley—or Hux—and last but not least, Jake." In return, I get a mix of chin lifts, grins, and nods. "And Walker is probably working somewhere, so you'll meet him at dinner."

"You *all* live here too?"

"Yep," they reply in unison.

"What about jobs?" I blurt out, my reporter instincts taking over.

Brady chuckles. "So we all share the load around the homestead. But some have jobs off the mountain too."

"What kind of jobs?" *Dammit, Faith. Stop working for once.*

"This and that." He points around the group. "Nash works as a cop in Kodiak for six weeks at a time, then he's home for two." *Whoa.* "Mase and Miller do construction around the district. Hux is a computer wiz, Nash trades renewable energy stocks online in his spare time, Micah is a lawyer, Tate is an ex-army medic, and Jake teachers at the local high school." Holy double whoa.

"And Walker?"

All the guys look at each other. "Walker does anything and everything."

"Hey, Nash," Brady says. "Can you show Faith where the guest cabin is?"

I lift a hand to still him. "Seriously, I'm good with directions. If you could just point me in the right direction, I'm sure to find it."

"Yeah. Not in these woods," Jake says. "Knowing our luck, you'll get lost and then Rena will have our butts for breakfast."

Serena laughs. "Or more like I won't make you my blueberry waffles."

A chorus of "Ooooh's" and "Burn!" erupts from the guys, making me smile. I love how they all seem to have adopted my bestie, and in turn, she's coming into her own. But I'm under deadline and I really need to get to my cabin so I can sneak in an hour or two of writing before dinner. What I didn't tell Rena was that I could only get here for three days instead of overnight because I promised my editor two stories while I was away. *Damn buttmunch.*

"Fine. Nash can take me. But, Serena..." I start, stepping up and stealing her away from Brady for a big bear hug. "I just need a couple of hours and then I'm all yours for the night." *Until I get back to my cabin and write again, anyway.*

She narrows her eyes at me; her gaze roaming my face before she sighs, her lips twitching at the side. "You're totally going to work right now."

"Yep," I say with a sigh. "But *then* I'm all yours."

Serena holds out her little finger for me, and I curl mine around it, the same way we've always done. "Pinky promise?"

"Pinky promise. Now, go with Brady and *relax*." I lean down and drop my voice so only she can hear. "Go have some naked fun." She grins and there's a light in her eyes telling me that's *exactly* what she's going to do.

"OK," she says. "But I'll see you at the Den at six? Does that work?"

I check my watch. "Perfect. Right, Nash. Let's go."

"Be back," he grunts to everyone before stepping up and snatching my suitcase from me.

"Oh. OK," I say, releasing the handle before I turn back to Serena and wave. "See you at dinner."

The entire walk along a well-worn dirt path, Nash doesn't talk. It weirds me out a little, so my need to fill the space between us with something takes over.

"So, you lived here long?" I ask.

"Long enough." It comes out as more of a grunt. *OK then.*

"Your brothers seem nice. Typical mountain men and all."

He quirks a brow. "You met many mountain men?"

"Well *no*, but—"

"Do you know what typical mountain men look like?"

"Again...No..." I sneak a glance his way and find him smirking. "You're screwing with me, aren't you!"

"Yep." He flashes a broad grin my way. "Had ya going there for a bit."

Dammit. He did.

"So, is this Walker just like the rest of you?"

"He's a workaholic these days. Keeps trying to prove himself when he doesn't need to."

"Why's that?" I ask.

"Call it a chip on his shoulder, I guess. Doesn't matter how many times we tell him, he's determined to show Brady he's ready to take the helm."

"You have a ship?"

Nash chuckles. "No. Take over from Brady as the leader of the Homestead."

"You guys have a leader?"

"Has Rena not talked about us?"

"Well yeah."

"Then you know." *Well, I thought I did...*

I open my mouth to ask more—call it the curse of being a journalist—but Nash comes to a stop and points to a row of cabins fifty feet ahead. "That's your home away from home."

"The one in the middle?"

"On the right. You got it from here?"

"Yeah. Don't think I'll get lost. Thanks for showing me the way and uh...for the *chat*."

He snickers and shakes his head. "Not much of a talker, sorry."

"Yeah. See, I *am* a talker."

"Guessed. That's how I know you weren't sent for me."

"Huh?"

"Dinner's at six." He gives me a nod, then turns back the way we came.

"OK. Well, I guess I'll see you at dinner then?"

He just grunts and waves over his shoulder, so I stand there for a second, watching him walk away before I turn and roll my bag behind me toward the cutest little cabin I've ever seen. My suitcase bangs against each of the two rustic wooden steps leading to a small porch, and I can imagine sitting out here with a cup of tea and my laptop, finding *all* the words I need to complete my stories.

With that in mind, I turn the handle on the door, but it seems a little stiff. So I bump it with my shoulder on my next attempt and suddenly it bursts open, sending me tumbling onto a rug on the floor inside.

“Oww, shit.” I’m literally upside down in a ball with my ass in the air, and it takes a concerted effort to untangle my limbs and roll over onto my back.

“What the actual fuck?” A deep gruff voice shouts, startling me as his face comes into view, a foreboding figure frowning down at me. And I’m sure there’s a very reasonable explanation for this man being here and yelling at me, but I’ve just taken a little tumble and I’m not really feeling myself, so all I can do is act on instinct.

I open my mouth and scream.

2

WALKER

All I wanted was five minutes of shut-eye before I went back out to work. I've been going nonstop since dawn, getting things ready for wedding guests and dealing with a compost issue. On top of that, I didn't want to stink up the place when Serena's friend got here. So I swung by my cabin and took a quick shower. Then I just sat down, closed my eyes, and the next thing I know I'm being invaded by the fucking tumblers from Cirque du Soleil. Seriously, who somersaults through a door that isn't even theirs?

And now she's screaming at me. *Brilliant*.

I stand with my hands on my hips, waiting till the screaming banshee calms down. If ever a man needed a wake-up call, it's this. I will *never* rest during the workday again.

"Finished?" I ask when she finally pauses for breath.

She scrambles to her feet and holds out a hand in defense. "That depends on what you plan to do to me."

"Why in the mountain's name would I ever do something to you? What the hell kind of life have you been living, woman?"

She moves her hand slightly as she drops her eyes then lifts them back up to meet mine. "A life where strange men aren't waiting for me *naked* in my cabin."

"What?" I glance down and fuck me dead, I'm not wearing any pants. *Guess I was more tired than I gave myself credit for.* "Oh, fuck." I cup my hand over my cock and balls then make a beeline for my closet, grabbing a pair of sweats and dragging them up my legs while she keeps her back to me. "For what it's worth, this is actually my cabin. I wasn't expecting a visitor."

"Huh?" She glances at me over her shoulder, turning fully when she spots me pulling a T-shirt over my head. "Nash told me this was it. Middle, right."

"You might want to check your bearings a little there. My cabin is the middle left, yours—Faith, I assume—is next door." I point to the direction of the guest cabin we spent most of the morning cleaning out. We don't get a huge amount of visitors up here on the mountain, so the spare cabin can get pretty messed up from disuse. Even worse, when a critter gets in there and tries to make a home. That can be a right pain to deal with.

"I see." Faith presses her lips together as she nods slowly and looks around. "This is *your* cabin. And mine is..."

"Over there." I give her a slight grin, starting to see the absurdity of the situation.

"Excellent." She takes a step back but then pauses. "Do you...do you think we could keep this between ourselves? I'm sorry for the racket I caused coming in here, and for accusing you, and looking at your...er..." Her eyes drop to my crotch area as her cheeks get even pinker than they already are. "Never mind. I'm just...I'm sorry. I should go." She thumbs over her shoulder then picks up her suitcase, stepping for the door with an awkward spin on her heel.

"Wait." She pauses, curiosity in her eyes as she turns my way. "We haven't officially met yet. I'm Walker," I say, stepping close to her and extending my hand.

"Faith," she practically whispers, about to slip her hand in mine before she winces. "You already knew that though, didn't you? I'm sorry. I've made a huge mess of this. It's just I've got a lot on my mind and it was a long drive, and I—sorry, I'm rambling. Again."

"It's fine. We can pretend nothing ever happened, and if anyone heard your scream, tell them it was a spider," I say with a wink, wrapping my big hand around hers, and that's when it happens. *Thump. Thump. Thump.* My heart hammers against my chest, jolting me with something I've never experienced before. It's like a charge of electricity or a fall that knocks the wind out of you. It takes a moment for me to catch my breath, and when I find Faith's eyes, they're wide and a little wild, meaning...*did she feel it too?*

"What the hell?" she says, snatching her hand back. "What just happened?"

A huge smile takes over my face as my eyes rake over her. She's luminous now. Not in a weird literal glowing way, but in a see-her-with-new-eyes kind of way. The shock from having her roll in through my door and catch me napping naked stopped me from *really* looking at her. I hadn't even registered how beautiful she is, with her long raven hair and her piercing blue eyes and slender body. She's tall too. Probably five-eleven if I were to hazard a guess, and she's just curvy enough that I'm grateful for the fact I'm wearing pants now. *Whoa.*

"Hello?" Faith waves a delicate hand in front of my face, making me realize I'm probably making her uncomfortable with my staring.

"Static electricity," I say quickly, clearing my throat.

"You think that was static electricity?" she asks, frowning at me, seeming somewhat amused.

"What else would you call it?" I ask, feigning ignorance because I don't want to scare her away by claiming the mountain just told me she's mine. We just met, and even I—a man who grew up hearing the stories of the mountain's call—know it sounds crazy to talk like that. My lips tip. "If I say there's obviously a *spark* between us, you'd *really* think I was a creep."

"Sounds crazy, but I kind of think that felt like the mountain's call," she says, freaking me the fuck out because that's the last thing I thought she'd say. She tilts her head, her beautiful blue eyes captivating in their curiosity. But seriously...

"What the hell do you know about the call?" I ask, wondering what kind of witchcraft this is.

"Aster Hollingsworth's books told me about it. They're Serena's favorites. She got me onto them in college."

"So you know?" I frown, not sure how I feel about this happening right now with Serena's best friend. I mean, I haven't fully proven myself as the head of the Homestead yet. Do I even deserve this honor yet?

"I do."

"And you felt it?"

She smiles. "I did."

"And what do we do about it?"

"Aren't you the mountain man? Shouldn't you know?" She laughs a little as she continues to study me.

"Brady's the only one of us who's gone through it. I haven't got a fucking clue."

"Well then, I guess we just play it by ear. I'll see you at dinner?" She steps toward the door, her bag in hand.

"Ah...yeah," I say, running a hand through my still-damp hair. "I'll see you at dinner."

With a final smile my way, she's gone, leaving me standing in the middle of my living area, wondering what the hell just happened. My brothers and I have been waiting for the mountain's call for so long, but we all failed to learn exactly how it works or what we're supposed to do. Thankfully, the wedding this weekend means the Coopers from Moose Mountain will be visiting. I'll ask my questions, and then I can formulate a plan so I don't fuck this up. I've fucked up a fair few things in my time, but this is important. After the homestead, it's the only other thing I need to get right.

3

FAITH

Since coming to the *right* cabin, I've unpacked my clothes and freshened up after the drive. Then I set up my workstation on the small round dining table near the cute kitchenette and sat down to start writing. That was my intention anyway. Instead, my laptop decided to do an update which wasted another twenty minutes, in which time I was alternating between staring out the window and reveling in the beauty of the Bear Mountain scenery. I admit to also closing my eyes and reliving the moment I first saw Walker Cooper—and I mean, saw *all of him*. His little flush of embarrassment was adorable but unnecessary because from what I saw, he has *nothing* to be embarrassed about. Like *at all*. I'm fanning myself just thinking about what he's packing.

When my computer finally starts working, it takes me another half hour to get the satellite internet to connect, and by then, my mind has drifted on to that *spark* I felt with Walker. So instead of working like I'm supposed to, I fall down the rabbit hole of internet searches and message boards while researching the Moose Mountain books and the premise behind them and this mountain call.

According to Aster Hollingsworth's website, the Cooper men living on Moose Mountain were the first to 'hear the call' after years of living and protecting the mountain. One by one, those four Cooper men fell for their one and only love as they came to the mountain and the nearby town and never left. Then there were the Cooper cousins—six, in fact—who also came back to the mountain one by one and met their soulmates. Martie—the only Cooper girl—lives here on Bear mountain with her husband Van and their daughter Vera. Her and Van fulfilled a prophecy that enabled the founding sons here in the homestead to hear the mountain's call after a long wait.

If I hadn't watched my best friend in the whole world come out of her shell and blossom like the rose she was always destined to be, then I would write of this magical mountain mumbo jumbo as total fantasy.

But my entire skin was electrified when Walker's hand touched mine. My heart started beating so hard against my chest I could *hear* it in my ears. And my entire body felt jolted, like when you're watching a world event unfold and you know your life will never be the same again.

So that *had* to be the call, right? I mean, what else could it be? It was too powerful to be something as simple as 'static electricity'. *Right?*

The more I read and research, the crazier and more doubtful I feel.

Unfortunately, I have no more time to delve into any of that because with thirty minutes to go before dinner, buttmunch sends me an email demanding I rewrite almost *all* of my story about a new community center in a poor neighborhood back in Anchorage. I'm fighting anger, annoyance, and frustration.

I know I can do so much better than the Anchorage Press, but I like it there—apart from buttmunch. I swear he sits in his lonely apartment at night and dreams up all the ways he can make my day hell.

My submitted story was relevant, emotive, and packed a lot of punch considering the short word count I was given. And most importantly, I'd made it my own. But *apparently*, it's superficial, wishy-washy, and my writing is '*too* invested' for a short news piece.

Having lost another five minutes just calming myself down so I don't chuck my laptop out this cute little cabin's window, I'm now multitasking—getting ready while also dictating my story. I'm throwing clothes off and on and trying to do my makeup while talking to my computer and watching the words coming out of my mouth populate on the screen. It'll need tidying up —especially after my little curse-filled tirade when my mascara wand decides to attack my eye—but I power through, silently wishing for the day when I can work for myself, on my own stories, without crazy deadlines and last-minute buttmunch-mandated changes.

"Full stop. End," I say with two minutes to spare, and a rather messy, but completely passable draft is now done. I'm also groomed, made up, and once I've slipped my favorite sling-back flats on my feet, I'll be ready to commence my Maid of Honor duties. I'm wearing a soft pink floral maxi dress with a cut out back, long sleeves and a skirt that kisses the floor. It's feminine and *slightly* flirty, but mainly just pretty and makes my mood lift immediately. A quick spray of perfume and one last look in the mirror, and I'm ready. I grab a coat and I'm out the door, destination The Den for a sit-down rehearsal dinner and then catching up with Serena.

"Fancy seeing you here?" a deep gruff voice I recognize says from behind me. I'm so in my head and focused on getting to the dinner only a little bit late, that I didn't even see him coming. *Then again, that mountain's call was an unexpected development too.* I stop on the salted path and turn to face a soft-eyed Walker grinning at me, then his gaze moves down my body like a caress before ever-so-slowly perusing me back up again until he reaches my face again. "Damn. You look amazing." My cheeks heat and I suddenly feel bashful, but I can't stop the chuffed smile curving my lips.

"I'm in a giant coat, but thank you, Walker." I check him out too. *I mean, that's fair, right?* He's slicked his hair back, but it still has that 'unruly, run your hands through it' look going for it, and his beard looks neat and tamed. His thick jacket is open enough that I can see a green shirt casually buttoned so I can see the hard curve of his pecks peeking through. "That green really sets off your, uh, eyes," I say, trying to give a reason for the way my eyes just linger right there on his chest. Suddenly, I have a clear understanding of man's obsession with cleavage. A nice man chest is just as alluring to us females. And don't get me started on the dark-denim jeans that cling to his hips before dropping in a straight line to polished black work boots. If mountain men weren't my thing before, they *definitely* are now. Or maybe it's just a *Walker* thing. Or a 'mountain's call' thing. Whatever *thing* it is, I'm feeling it. All over. Everywhere. And I like it. *I can't look away.*

All of a sudden, it's like we both realize we're just standing there staring and smiling at each other. *Shit. This is awesome and awkward and weirdly comfortable, all at the same time.*

"Um—"

"Right. Shall we—"

We both talk over each other and a giggle escapes my mouth.

"Let's try that again," Walker says with a smile as he extends his hand. "Can I walk you to dinner?"

My smile widens, and I dip my head. "You may." I slide my fingers between his, that zing sparking to life between us again as my pulse speeds up. *This is* not *static electricity.*

Walker leans in and brings his mouth close to my ear. "I felt it that time too, sweetheart. I think it's just going to keep happening to us. Maybe we should just run with it." Then he takes a slow breath in and he straightens again, giving my hand a gentle squeeze. "Fuck, you smell amazing by the way. Especially in the crook of your neck. It's intoxicating."

I tilt my head and give him a wink. "Maybe I'm an enchantress..." I whisper, my mind reeling after all he just said.

"Of that, I have absolutely no doubt." He lifts his arm, bringing my knuckles to his lips and pressing a barely there kiss to my skin, causing goosebumps to appear in his wake. "Let's get the maid of honor to dinner, shall we?"

"You're pretty important there too, you know?"

Walker shakes his head as we make our way down the path. "I'm working on it. But tonight is about Brady and Serena. He's the first of the founding sons to get married and find his true love. He's the leader, and I'm trying but failing to fill his boots."

"Why do you have to fill his boots at all? Can't all the founding brothers run this place together?"

A slight smirk tips up the side of his mouth and sends happy butterflies dancing about in my belly. "Absolutely. And we do. But every group needs a leader, and with Brady's attention divided between the homestead and Serena, I have to earn my place. I'm the baby brother, so I have more ground to make up than the others."

"Why's that? You seem pretty impressive to me?"

He snorts. "Are you saying that because you saw my twig and berries?" I cover my mouth and bite my lip, trying so hard not to laugh at that, but it's too funny, and since we're the only two that know about it—hopefully—I can't stop the snicker from coming out.

"It's more like a *trunk*, actually," I mutter.

"What was that?

"Nothing," I quickly blurt out. "Anyway, I thought we weren't going to speak of that again?"

"Ah, it's just between us." Walker's lips twitch and he winks. "And the mountain spirit. At least you're laughing about it now, and not back then. I'm not sure my ego could've handled a beautiful woman giggling at me in my birthday suit."

"Believe me, you have *nothing* to laugh at," I blurt out before I gasp and try to jerk my hand out of his grasp to cover my mouth.

Walker chuckles and tightens his grip on my hand. "Nuh-uh, sweetheart. You don't get to give me a glimpse of that firecracker personality I knew was inside you, then hide it away again. You can be yourself around me, swear to god. Actually, you should *only* be yourself around me, and I promise to do the same for you. Deal?"

"Deal." My heart swells in my chest as I swoon at his words. *Walker Long is as smooth as they come, I'll give him that.*

He grins at me, his eyes glittering as he tugs me a little closer and we continue on. It feels so natural and right walking along with my hand in his, but the moment is broken into by the chime of a cell phone coming from Walker's pants pocket. "Shit. I'm so sorry. I just need to check this. I'm kind of on duty tonight."

"Duty?" I ask as he releases my hand and digs out the phone. His brows furrowing deeper as he scans the message.

He meets my eyes and I know our walk has just come to an unfortunate and premature end. "Yeah. Look, I'm sorry, but I've just gotta go check something before dinner. I'll take you to the door, then I'll catch up with you when I get back. Is that OK?"

"Absolutely, Walker. I can take it from here if you li—"

"Nope. My Mama raised me to be a gentleman, and although you're as safe as you can be on this mountain and in the homestead, I'll take you to the Den and then I promise to seek you out later." I look down to realize that somehow we're facing each other now and he's holding both my hands in his.

I swoon a little at the fact he's still going to walk me to the door, because whatever he has to do must be important if he's going to be late to his brother's pre-wedding celebration, right? And also, he's checking if that's OK with me. I mean, is this guy real? Because he seems too good to be true.

"You're a good man, Walker Long."

"As long as you think that, Faith, I think I could believe it too."

We start moving again, and a minute later, we're standing outside The Den.

Walker is all business now, and even though I know he said he's coming back as soon as he can, I'm already feeling a little bereft.

"Save me a dance for later, sweetheart," he says, surprising me. His tone is soft and low, and although there are others milling around outside the building, I know he said that just for me. Then he squeezes my hand before letting it go. But in the blink of an eye, he's gone.

After dinner and speeches, Serena hooks her arm in mine and never lets me out of her sight. She takes me around to every single resident and introduces me. The more people I meet, the more I wish I could stay here longer. The entire concept of the homestead intrigued me before I came here. Every time she'd call me, Serena would tell me all about their environmentally friendly practices, their use of renewable resources, and how they all work and live harmoniously together for the greater good of the mountain. Now that I've come to visit, and I've met the residents, I'm officially fascinated. I can't wait till tomorrow when I can go up to the mountaintop. And then on Sunday, if Serena is too busy in honeymoon-bliss with her new husband, there's all those founding sons to show me around. Maybe Walker, if I can ever find that man again. There's this weird empty sort of feeling knowing he's not here. It's not pain, it's not even an ache. It's more like how it feels when you get a dull cramp in your leg.

I've tried to be discreet, but I keep looking for him whenever Serena and I move around the room. I start to wonder if Walker cut out on dinner because he didn't want to be here, although going by what Nash said earlier, it doesn't seem like the kind of thing he'd do.

Speaking of Nash, he's missing in action too. I look over at the table where all the other founding sons are sitting a.k.a. the hottie's table, and there's another one missing. What's happening? It's like they're vanishing into the cold mountain air, one hottie at a time. *There must be something big going on.*

"C'mon, Faith. You have to meet Gandalf."

"Gandalf? As in—"

Serena rolls her eyes. "His name is Tim, but Brady and the guys all call him Gandalf. He hates it but loves it all at the same time, I swear."

I scrunch my face up in confusion. This place keeps getting stranger, and weirder, yet somehow *cooler* the more I find out about it. It would be such an awesome writer's retreat location. *I wonder if they've ever thought of adding another income stream*, I think to myself, as the cogs in my brain start working overtime. Then I'm snapped from my thoughts when Serena is tugging on my arm and we're walking toward a bearded, silver-haired, wizard-looking tall man with headphones covering his ears and a Metallica song blasting from the speakers. Supposedly he's some wise man prophet, but to my eyes, he's hilariously cool. I love it!

By the end of the night, Gandalf starts to play slow songs to wind things down. One by one, the residents are starting to make their way back to their cabins, preparing for the big day of celebrations tomorrow.

Worse still, Walker never returned. So all that anticipation for a dance with the man I've *apparently* been called here for was for nothing. And with the wedding tomorrow and all the lead up to that, and being Serena's right-hand lady for *everything*, I doubt I'll have time to catch up with him the entire day. Which only leaves Sunday, and that's my last day on Bear Mountain before I have to reluctantly leave and go back to my life in Anchorage. That doesn't seem fair...

Maybe the mountain's call is all smoke and mirrors and *is* actually fictional. As much as I'd like to believe that I was predestined to find my one and only true love, surely if that was the case, I'd at least get the chance to *talk* to him...or get to know him a bit more. Maybe have that dance he made a point of asking for. You know, *dating*-like things.

With a resigned sigh, I wave my goodbyes, kiss Serena on the cheek, and tell Brady not to wear her out too much before the big day, earning a blush from my best friend. Then I make my way back to my cute little cabin and yawn at the idea of having to stay up and write the story I didn't get to earlier because *buttmunch* was being a typical ass. I guess a hard day's work is never done, even on the magical mountain.

At least tomorrow, I get to watch my best friend and soul sister marrying the love of her life. Even if the mountain *did* get it wrong with me and it's call, it got it right with Serena, and that's enough for me.

Now if this *thump. thump. thump* of my heart would quieten down. Maybe I can get some sleep.

4

WALKER

After getting a weather alert that a snow squall is headed our way, I race up to the sacred spring to secure the archway and seating we'd spent fucking hours setting up earlier today. The wedding needs to go off without a hitch and we don't need a freak weather event ruining it for us—not when the ceremony is *my* responsibility. I've let Brady and Serena down in the past, and I don't want to do it again.

"Nash, I need you up here," I yell into my cell as the wind howls around me. I'm fighting a losing battle as I try to tie everything down. A stack of chairs just blew straight past me, and I think I may have bitten off more than I can chew.

The sacred spring is a sheltered space that is rarely affected by snow and storms, but this squall is the perfect size and ferocity to break through the tree line and coat the heated space with a layer of icy snow. At best, we're gonna have a ground coated in slush come morning. *Fabulous.*

"I'm on my way. Gonna bring Jake too. Many hands make light work and all that," he says, and I can make out the Gandalf-spun music in the background. I'm cursing the fact that I'm missing the dinner *and* the dancing this evening. I wanted the chance to explore this connection I have with Faith, but the more the weather rallies against me, the more I think that maybe I was wrong. Maybe the feelings I'm having toward Faith are just basal desires and not the mountain's call at all. Or maybe I'm just reading into it too much?

"We'll probably need it. The wind up here is nuts. Gonna need to redo everything come morning."

"That sucks. OK. We're leaving now."

"Thanks, mate."

I do as much as I can while I wait for Nash and Jake to show, and once they turn up, we work together, rolling up silk ribbons, folding and securing chairs, and dismantling the archway and the dais. We tie everything down, making sure nothing can blow away. But by the time we're done, the rehearsal dinner is well and truly over.

"Rum?" Nash pulls a flask from inside his coat, passing it to me as we carefully walk back down the mountain. The snowfall is getting thicker and the air colder, so the perceived warmth in my belly is a welcomed treat.

“Thanks,” I say, tipping the flask back and filling my mouth. “I needed that.” The heat pools and spreads like tendrils, relaxing me as we traverse the icy path back to the homestead.

“You seem quiet,” Jake points out when I pass the flask to him.

“We missed the rehearsal,” I say.

“It was just a dinner,” Nash replies. “Really, it’s just an excuse for a party.”

“I know. I just…had plans.”

“Plans?” Jake frowns as he looks my way.

“Ohhh.” Nash claps his hand on my bag then squeezes my shoulder. “You met Faith, didn’t you?”

“Met her,” I say, wondering when Nash learned to read minds. “And I think the mountain called her to me. But it’s hard to be sure when I’m too busy fucking about with chairs instead of spending the night dancing with her.”

“Dancing?” Jake’s eyes widen and he laughs. “Oh, man. You’ve got it bad already. How long have you known this girl?”

"Minutes," I say, my voice flat. "She walked into my cabin instead of hers. Scared the shit out of me while I was taking a nap."

"Oh, shit." Nash laughs. "I did that once. Found you sleeping naked."

"You mean you *don't* sleep naked?" Jake asks his brother. "When do your balls ever get to be free?"

"When they're tapping against your girlfriend's throat," Nash throws back, causing us to freeze and look at him like he's got two heads.

"That's fucked up, Nash," I say. "Cause we all know Jake's girlfriend is his right hand."

"Screw you, Walk," Jake retorts, flipping me the bird. "For your information, my 'girlfriend' is of the inflatable variety. If Nash is tapping her then that shit's just unhygienic."

His comment sends us into a fit of laughter and starts another round of locker room banter that carries on until we reach the homestead.

"Why don't you go see her?" Nash says after I thank him and Jake for leaving the party to come help me.

"It's late." I shrug. "And she's probably pissed I stood her up."

"Well," Jake says as he rubs his hands together and blows his breath between them. "By my count, you've got about sixty hours to decide if she's your One before she leaves on Monday. And if she's already seen your junk and didn't run away screaming, I reckon *that's* a sign in itself. I wouldn't waste any time if I were you."

I scowl. "No one said she saw my junk."

"Whatever, man. That shit is between you and her. My point is, if you like her and you felt the call, there isn't any time to waste. Seize the day. Seize the moment. Go find out if she's the girl the mountain brought to you or spend the rest of your life wondering."

"I know what I'd do," Nash says, nodding as he meets my eyes.

"OK," I say. "I'll go see her. But if this goes bad, I'm blaming you, and you." I give them both a pointed look and they laugh.

"Fine by me," Nash says. "But I get to be best man if you two get married."

"Hey!" Jake socks him in the arm. "I gave the pep talk. I should be the best man."

And it's with that argument still going that I leave them, my feet pointed solidly in the direction of Faith's cabin. "Just give me a sign," I say the mountain, shivering when a gust of wind whirls around me just as I turn the corner and spot the soft light shining through Faith's cabin window. That's when I know my mountain has given me one.

5

FAITH

I'm knee-deep in story mode. Jewel is playing on my Bluetooth speaker, my fingers are moving a mile a minute, I'm wearing my a-typical writing wear, and I have a bucket-load of coffee within reach in case I end up pulling an all-nighter to get my work done.

Buttmunch replied to me with only a few minor changes to my community center story—thank god—but then he sends me another one to write for *Wednesday's* edition which immediately cancels out my relief that *maybe* I could enjoy the rest of my time at the homestead instead of working every spare moment I get.

Then there's Walker. The mysterious, intriguing man who has me thinking about him a little bit too much in less than a day. From our rather unique first meeting, and then our conversation on the way to dinner, my entire body warms at the mere thought of him, despite the coldness of the snow falling outside. I've even caught myself getting distracted while thinking about him and doodling his name down in my notebook instead of focusing on work like I should.

I take a big gulp of my coffee and wrap my blanket a little tighter around me as I try to talk myself into staying awake and writing about Mabel Jenkins, a hilarious little old lady I met in Kodiak who still volunteers at the city's public library two mornings a week, despite turning one hundred last month. I've drafted the outline of the human interest story, and I'm just about to go back through it and add in Mabel's funny quips and life advice she was more than happy to hand down to me when there's a knock at the door.

A glance at the time on my computer shows it's late—almost eleven. Figuring it could only be Serena, I jump up, not caring if my bestie sees me in sweatpants, a tank top, my favorite UAA hoodie, bright pink fluffy slippers, and my hair coiled on top of my head with a pencil stuck in it—it's my thinking knot—because it wouldn't be the first time she's seen my look like a train wreck on deadline.

"Hey, babe. What are you—" My breath catches when I find Walker leaning against the doorframe, his coat covered in a dusting of snow, his eyes soft and lazy as they slowly look me over before a slow smile curves his lips.

"Now *that's* an outfit," he says, taking a step toward me. "And it might just be my favorite look on you." My eyes widen as I move back to make room for him. He knocks the snow off his coat and boots, taking them both off while he steps inside. His hooded gaze never leaves mine as he closes the door behind him and hangs his coat on the hook by the entry. *He's obviously planning on staying a while...*

I cross my arms over my chest, feeling rather under-dressed—or maybe I'm *too* dressed—for the feelings suddenly coursing through me. Shock, surprise, embarrassment, relief, happiness, elation...*lust*.

"I thought you'd ran away," I whisper.

"Yeah. I'm sorry I didn't make it to the dinner. I got news that this weather system was moving in and we'd spent a lot of time setting up the mountain top for the ceremony tomorrow, and I didn't want it to be ruined."

"Aww, Walker. That's so sweet."

"It's the least I can do. A couple's wedding day is one of the most important and memorable moments in their lives together, so if I can help make sure it runs smoothly, there's nothing I wouldn't do to make sure Brady and Serena start their marriage together on a good note." His lips curve up into a sexy smile. *God. This man is something else. There's no way I can resist him.*

Walker looks over at my computer, his face falling. "Oh, did I disturb you? I can go if you like."

"No!" I blurt out, my heart pounding. "No." I keep my voice softer this time. "I don't want you to go. I was just trying to get ahead now so I don't fall behind while I'm doing wedding stuff."

Walker tilts his head. "Your boss didn't let you take vacation time?"

"Barely...my editor is kind of a hardass and I'm not his favorite person, so I have a few stories to submit while I'm away."

"He's making you work on vacation?" he growls, his tone rough and menacing, the mood in the room going wired. It's so unlike anything I'd expect from him, that I jump a little in shock.

"It's OK," I say quietly. "He does this all the time. He didn't like that management appointed as a *paid* intern, so he rides me hard to make sure he gets his money's worth."

"If you don't like something *management* does, You take it up with management. You don't take it out on young, beautiful, *driven* women like you who have a passion for what they do and work their asses off doing what they love." My lips part and I stare at him, seeing a whole new, even better, side to this man—and I already liked all the parts I'd seen of him so far. He's angry *for me*. This man I've just met is being protective, and it might just be the sexiest thing I've ever seen on *any* man.

It makes me want to jump into his arms and never let go.

I close the distance between us and place my hand on his arm, not surprised this time when I feel that now-familiar zing spark between us. "It's nothing I can't handle, Walker. It just makes me work harder and I'm more determined to prove to him that I deserve to be there, and I can write kick ass stories that move people, that touch them in here," I say, resting my fingers over his thumping heart. "That's not to say I don't appreciate your protectiveness, though."

"You're one of the most amazing women I've ever met. Do you know that?" he rasps.

"I do now," I whisper, leaning in. "But honestly, you didn't have to explain."

"But I did, because I asked you to save me a dance, and since I was looking forward to holding you in my arms and dancing to Gandalf's *awesome* music, I was disappointed I'd missed out."

"We can dance tomorrow at the wedding reception," I say, happy that we're going to have the chance for a do-over."

"There's music playing now," he says, as *You Were Meant For Me* starts crooning out of the speaker.

"There sure is," I say, my heart galloping in my chest in anticipation.

Grinning, Walker reaches out and frames my hips with his hands. “May I have this dance, sweetheart?”

Lord, save me. I’m swooning. How can I dance with the man if I don't trust my body not to melt into a puddle on the floor?

I tilt my head and smile, gliding my hands to loop behind his head, both of us meeting in the middle, bringing our bodies close together as we sway side to side to Jewel’s angelic voice. The lyrics fill the air, but soon they fade away and it’s just the two of us staring deep into each other's eyes, my soul feeling so at ease and comfortable.

“I like dancing with you,” I murmur, resting my head on Walker’s shoulder.

“Me too.” His hand drifts up to rub slow circles on my back. “I wouldn’t wanna be anywhere else right now.”

We stay like that in each other's arms for what seems like forever. But far too soon for my liking, the music stops playing, my speaker beeping and announcing it has a low battery.

“It’s getting late, sweetheart, and we’ve all got a big day tomorrow,” he murmurs, his warm soft gaze drifting down to focus on my mouth. I pout, which makes his eyes crinkle at the sides. He lifts his hands to cup my cheeks. “Damn, you’re cute. Totally fucking adorable.”

“You’re not too bad yourself.”

He looks around my face, his tongue darting out to wet his lips. God, I want him to kiss me. "You make me feel things I didn't think I was ready for."

"And now?"

"You make me think I can do anything and everything as long as you're by my side." His tone is so rough and guttural it washes over me like a warm fuzzy blanket that I never want to let go of.

"I like this," I say, leaning against him, feeling like he's got me and trusting he'd never let me go. "I like *you*."

"Good. Because I like you too." He dips his head and I hold my breath as he runs the tip of his nose alongside mine. "And I love the way you dance, and smell, and laugh." He presses his lips to my cheek and holds them there, letting me feel his smile against my skin. "And the way you make me feel like the king of the mountain just because I got to hold you in my arms."

Woman down. I'm done for. I'm ready to give up everything just to stay like I am right here, right now, with this magnificent mountain man. *If only...*

With one last kiss on my cheek, he straightens, his gaze going hooded when I don't even try to hide my disappointment that this moment is over.

He drags his thumb over my lips, his eyes following the movement.

"I'll let you get back to your work. But thank you for making this a night I won't forget." He slowly shifts back, his hands dropping away.

I scrunch my nose up as I watch him slide his coat back on over his shoulders. "It was just a dance, though."

"No, Faith. It could never be *just* a dance between you and me. Everything that happens between us means something so much more. I know it, the mountain knows it, and whatever it takes, however long it takes for *you* to know it, however long I have to wait to make you mine...Sweetheart, just know I'm all in."

I suck in my breath at his words, and with a lopsided smile that makes me want to rush and drag him back inside, he walks out the door, leaving me standing in the middle of the cabin in my hoodie, sweatpants, and with my pink fluffy slippers on my feet, frozen in place because Walker Long has just succeeded in knocking my world completely off-axis. I'm not even sure I want to right it.

6

WALKER

I'm up super early the morning of the wedding, clearing the ground around the sacred spring and setting up for the ceremony once again. That squall wreaked a lot of havoc in the secluded area, but with the help of my brothers, we get it looking just like new with time to spare—well, just enough to get back to the homestead and put our fancy suits on. I feel like a monkey in a penguin suit, but hey, it's my big brother's wedding. Wearing jeans, boots and a flannel ain't gonna cut it today.

Adjusting my tie, I take a look around the clearing from where I'm standing with the rest of the founding brothers up front as we wait for the ceremony to begin. There's chatter filling the air as homesteaders and friends—Serena's rancher friends made the trek up here too—fill the seats and wait for the bride to arrive.

“This is kind of eerie, don’t you think?” Nash asks, leaning close to my ear. “Like, some spirit living in the mountain decides who we spend our lives with and we all just go along with it.” He shakes his head, like he’s trying to wrap his thoughts around the notion.

“You don’t believe in the power of the mountain?” I ask, turning his way. Nash is a pragmatic person by nature, but I’ve gotta say, I’m surprised to hear him question the mountain’s choices that way. Especially when he was one of the few of us who never left her. He stayed here from birth to now, training as a local cop and dividing his time between working in Kenshaw and working on the Homestead.

“I do. I just...I don’t know, look at all the Coopers. They seem crazy happy. But is any of this real? Or is it just some sort of brainwashing we all eat up because it gives us something to believe in, something to hope for?”

Following his line of sight, I look over to where the Coopers sit. Martie—our Mountain’s mother—speaks enthusiastically to her brothers and cousins. Each of them sits close to their soulmate, always touching and smiling.

“They seem...blissful, content,” I say, bouncing a shoulder. “And if meeting Faith is anything to go by, it’s not a brainwashing situation. It’s just a feeling. Something that’s hard to understand unless you experience it for yourself.”

"I've heard the way Brady describes it, and a few of the Coopers have spoken openly about when they heard the call. But, I don't know man, it sounds a lot like anxiety."

"Anxiety?" I can't help but laugh. "Look at them, Nash. Do they look anxious to you? Or are they just happy and provided for, just like the mountain promised?"

Nash releases a grunt and turns away, leaving me to my thoughts as I continue to people watch. Martie is bouncing her daughter on her knee while Van absent-mindedly strokes the back of her neck and chats with Gray, the oldest and natural leader of the Cooper family. They are the original mountain family, where this whole 'call' business started. They reside on Moose Mountain where the first mother made a deal with the mountain spirit to watch over and protect it from the harm human's cause. In turn, the mountain spirit would provide everything they needed—food, shelter, love—so their lives would be complete and fulfilled as the protectors of the mountain. For a couple of generations, there were only sons born to the Cooper clan. But then Marta came along, the first Cooper-born daughter. Her birth coincided with the waking of Bear Mountain's spirit, and it was prophesied that she would one day come to Bear Mountain and start a family of her own, thereby bringing the Cooper family's bargain with her to the Bear Mountain spirit. When she had her first child, the call was activated. And we homestead brothers—the sons of the founding families who have spent years protecting the mountain simply because we care about it—are now being rewarded with their one true love.

The 'call' acts as a kind of magnet that reaches out across the nation, finding our soulmates and creating a spiritual urge inside them that makes them seek out the mountain and therefore us.

It's Pure Magic. The stuff of legends.

When we were kids, we heard about the mountain's call via our friends on Moose Mountain. It wasn't until we moved away then came back as adults when our parents left us the homestead that we met Tim—aka Gandalf—and learned about the prophecies involving Bear Mountain too. The old bastard knew we were all coming back before we did, and he was literally standing at the gates welcoming us all home. At first we thought he was crazy, but then he revealed himself as a relative of Moose Mountain's Cooper family and we realized that he was somehow connected to Bear Mountain spirit.

He's been guiding us ever since, and now he's presiding over this wedding, standing on the dais to welcome the very first bride called here by the mountain for a founding brother. It's an auspicious occasion, and one I'm more than excited about since this wedding is the reason Faith came here. The call was immediate and strong. So, with the weather report clear, there is nothing that can drag me away from her this time. Tonight is the night I let her know she's mine.

When Michael Bublé's *Can't Take My Eyes off You* plays over the speaker, the chatter instantly quiets and all heads turn toward the entrance of the clearing. Boone Cooper's daughter, Audrey heads the procession as the flower girl, accompanied by her cousin Rowan (Gray's son) as the page boy. Then it's a procession of bridesmaids, mostly picked from the friendships Serena has made on the Homestead and in town, and finally the woman my heart has been waiting for emerges. For a moment, I can't even breathe.

Faith makes her way up the aisle, smiling as she nods to the people she knows, looking like an absolute vision in a flowing lilac dress and a flower crown on the top of her head that matches the bouquet in her hands. Her lips are painted a dusty pink and her hair cascade in curls over her shoulders. And the best part? When her eyes find mine, they stay there. And suddenly I'm having visions of the day I get to be the guy preparing to say my vows and join my life with hers. Because it will happen. It's only a matter of time before she realized that this mountain is where she'll want to stay.

After Faith, of course, is Serena. She looks stunning in her white dress as her father escorts her up the aisle to where Brady waits with an eager smile. I'd love to be able to describe that moment in vivid detail, but the blood rushing in my ears and the heating of my skin has my eyes glued to Faith. My body is saying 'go get her' and I'm trying my best to maintain control so I'm not standing up here with a hard-on the size of Bear Mountain.

Vows are exchanged and words of love and devotion are spoken, but all I can do is think about devoting my life to the goddess across from me. She's everything I've ever wanted. For the first time in my life, I find myself wanting to be better than my best. She inspires me to work harder and strive higher, to prove to her that I'm the man she needs. I know we'll have some mountains of our own to scale since her job and family are in Anchorage and Kinleyville, and I'm up here, but this feeling can't be ignored. We need to be together. Come hell or high water, I'm going to make it happen.

Cheers erupt all around us, and it takes me a moment to realize that Brady and Serena are now husband and wife. When I start clapping, I lock eyes with Faith again and find her laughing.

"You're adorable," she mouths.

"You're beautiful," I mouth back. She blushes and my dick gets hard. *Shit.* "Save me a dance."

"OK." She nods, then laughs when Nash whistles through his fingers, and the founding brothers all cheer Brady and Serena on. Brady only kisses her harder, tilting her back until one of her feet lifts off the ground to maintain her balance. The congregation goes wild.

"I'd like to present to all of you, Mr. and Mrs. Brady and Serena Long. May the mountain guide you well," Gandalf says when Brady and Serena come up for air. They join hands and lift them about their heads as we cheer them on. Then they head back down the aisle, meaning the rest of us are to follow. And lucky me, I get to escort Faith back to the homestead.

"On second thoughts," I say as she slides her arm in mine. "I think I'll need to take up your entire dance card for the night."

"Is that right?" she giggles.

"It is. Normally, I'm a sharing man, but when it comes to my woman, I'm not inclined to share at all."

"Then I'll make sure I only dance with you, Walker Long. I hope you brought your dancing shoes because I intend to dance to *every* song."

"You weren't wrong when you said you wanted to dance to every song," I say, my arms firmly around Faith's waist as I hold her close. She has her head rested on my chest and I swear she's almost falling asleep in my arms. My feet hurt like a bitch, and Faith got rid of her heels hours ago, but every bit of discomfort is only minor when I get the chance to keep holding on to this beauty. I never want to let her go.

"And you weren't lying when you said you'd dance every one of them with me," she says, looking up at me and smiling. "I've had a wonderful time tonight."

Reaching up, I tuck her dark hair behind her ear, noticing the way the curl has almost dropped out entirely. The flower crown is somewhere on a table, and she looks just disheveled enough that I keep thinking about what it would be like to wake up next to her. To have her in my bed. To be the one to muss her up.

"Ready to get out of here?"

"I'd have left the moment we arrived if you'd asked," she replies quickly. And I can't help but laugh as I run my thumb back and forth along her cheekbone.

"You mean, I could have been ravishing you all this time?"

She quirks her brow. "I can neither confirm nor deny those allegations."

Sucking in a lungful of air, I smile as I lean in and brush my nose alongside hers. She releases a light gasp that I feel right between my legs. If I'm honest, dancing with her all night has been a sweet kind of torture. It's allowed me to touch her and learn about her body, pay attention to the way she reacts, the way she moves. It's a way of getting up close and intimate without taking things too fast in the direction of the bedroom.

I'm keenly aware of the pain Brady was in during his time away from Serena when she was unable to move to the mountain. And I know that the closer I get to Faith, the stronger the bond becomes between us, until we can't live without each other at all. As much as I want to fast forward to that point where I claim her and make her mine, I also know she's leaving in just two days. So there's a limit as to how close we can get before saying goodbye becomes impossible. And I'm not about to commit a felony forcing her to stay.

"Then let's get out of here," I say, swiping a bottle of champagne off one of the tables. "My feet are *killing* me."

She giggles and picks up her shoes from where she tossed them earlier. "I can't even begin to explain how strongly I hate the idea of putting my feet back in these things."

"Then don't," I say, handing her the champagne bottle.

"What am I going to do with this?" She looks from the bottle to me.

"You're gonna hold it while I carry you back to the cabin." She lets out a little squeak as I scoop her up in my arms and carry her toward the door, saying a quick goodbye to those who remain at the reception. Most of the guests—including the bride and groom—left long ago. It's just been the stalwart partiers and the old-timers who are determined to stick it out until the end.

“Are you cold?” Faith asks as I trudge from the den toward our cabins through the snow.

“No. You?” I ask, meeting her beautiful blue eyes.

“No,” she whispers. “I’m *very* warm.” Then she trails her fingers down the buttons of my dress shirt and I let out a groan. *Keep it in your pants, Walker.*

“I’m taking you to my cabin,” I say as we approach, deciding that I’m not interested in sleeping with any sort of wall between us. I need her with me for as long as I can have her.

“You want me to go inside your cabin when you haven’t even kissed me yet?” She feigns an indignant gasp. “Why, Walker. That’s very forward of you.”

I release a chuckle as I step up onto my porch and slowly lower her to the ground, her back resting against my closed door as I lean in and brace an arm against the wood. “You want me to kiss you first?”

She nods as she looks up at me and licks her lips. “I’ve been hoping you would all night.”

“Just all night?” I shift a little closer, placing my palm over her cheek and running my thumb back and forth over her skin. I love how soft and creamy it is, the way her cheeks flush pink the more I touch her. It makes me wonder how deep that blush goes. Is her sex throbbing for my touch the way my dick is for hers?

"Last night too," she admits, leaning her head into my palm. "Maybe even since I first busted into your cabin." Her blush grows deeper, and I just know she's picturing me naked right now. *Fucking brilliant.*

"Do you know what I've been thinking about, sweetheart?" She shakes her head and I shift a little closer, allowing my erection to press against her soft belly. "Seeing you. Naked." Dipping my head, I brush my mouth along the edge of her jaw, loving how she quivers beneath my hands.

"Well...fair's fair, I suppose. I did see you in all your glory."

"You think I'm glorious, huh?" I smile against her skin as I press my lips to her forehead.

"Impressive might be a better word," she blurts before her eyes go wide and lock with mine. My grin gets even wider.

"Impressive. That is a good word," I say, shifting my hand so my finger hooks beneath her chin, tilting her mouth up. "Where would you like me to kiss you first? Your mouth?" I brush my lips lightly to hers before dropping a kiss right at the corner. "Your cheeks?" I tilt her head to the side and drag my mouth to the apple of her cheek. "Your neck?" I lean down and suck gently on her delicate skin before I lift my head again. "Or do you want me to kiss you...lower?" I drop to my knees and slide my hands beneath her long dress, skirting my palms up the bare skin of her legs as her breathing quickens and I press a heated kiss against silky material at her stomach before I lift my eyes to hers. "Well?"

"Oh, Jesus Christ," she mutters before the bottle of champagne and her heels hit the porch and her arms go around my neck, and she's flinging herself at me, our mouths connecting in a clash of teeth and tongues. *Lips it is then.*

I push to my feet, lifting her with me, her legs automatically wrapping around my waist as I carry her through the door, and kick it closed behind me while I make a beeline for the bed. As I lower her down, I kiss her slow and deep, our tongues moving in harmony as tiny gasping mews leave her chest and deep rumbling groans leave mine. The urge to take more from her is stronger than I expected. I could lose myself entirely, just in her mouth.

"We need to slow down," I rasp, forcing my mouth from hers even though a mountain's worth of strength is begging me to keep going.

"We don't." She writhes beneath me, her hand finding its way between us and boldly cupping my bulge in her palm. "I want this."

"I do too," I strain, trying not to lose myself too much in the gentle rubbing of her hand. "But you're leaving on Monday. And we can't..." I place my hand on her wrist to stop her movement before I lose complete control. "We can't sleep together. Well, we can, just not in the way we're headed."

"But why?"

I look down at her confused eyes, regretting my words more and more with each second. "You've read the books. You know why."

"Because we'll be bonded," she whispers, her body relaxing beneath me. "I forgot about that part. I remember Serena was a mess after they... *got together* ...too soon."

Swallowing hard, I lean my forehead against hers. "I don't want to put us through that."

"OK. Then what would you like to do? Should I go back to my cabin?"

"No. I want you here. In my bed. I'd like to hold you and just...sleep...if that's OK?"

A slow smile creeps across her face as she nods and flattens her hands against my chest. "You're one of the good ones, Walker Long. Has anyone ever told you that?"

"Not that I recall," I say, since fuck up is the term that most often comes to mind. I've messed up more times than I can count. But this thing with Faith, that's something I need to get right.

"Well, you are. And if I can be so bold as to say so, I think I'm already falling for you."

I lean down and press my lips to hers in a soft kiss. "I'm falling for you too," I say, already dreading the fact that she's leaving so soon. *How am I supposed to be without this?*

7

FAITH

I slowly open my eyes, feeling so cozy and warm, I don't want to move, or get out of this bed, or leave this mountain. *Ever*.

My pillow is Walker's muscular chest and during the night, I've ended up plastered against his side, half lying on top of him, which is a *lot* different to the way we fell asleep with Walker spooned behind me, his strong arms wrapped around me, making me feel so cherished and protected. Despite wishing we'd gone further than we did last night, I'd fallen asleep within minutes.

Now I'm wide awake and a glance at Walker's slumbering body has me thinking all kinds of dirty things. I know he said we can't *be* together right now, but a little exploration should be OK. What else is a girl to do when she's in bed with a man who makes her blood heat and her heart race but explore?

Feeling bold and turned on, I run the flat of my hand over his chest, my fingers brushing through the dark hair covering his pecs as I marvel at how warm he feels and how *right* being here with him feels.

After checking he's still asleep, I dip my chin and brush my lips against his nipple, loving the huff of air that escapes his lips. Emboldened, I glide my palm down his torso, loving the feel of his smooth toned muscles under my touch and how they tense and contract the more my hands roam his body.

“Hmm,” he rumbles, his fingers moving to my hair. “Baby, you can wake me up with your hands any time you like.”

I turn my cheek and meet his hooded sleepy eyes. “Is that so?”

“Oh yeah,” he groans as I toy with the waistband of his boxer shorts. Then a surprised yelp escapes me as I’m hauled up over his body until I’m lying on top of him. He slants my head to the side before crashing his lips to mine, his tongue diving inside in an erotic dance that has my insides quivering. *Now this is a different way to dance with Walker.*

He shifts his legs, bending his knee so his thick thigh is pressing against my wet core. One of his hands moves to my butt, and as if my hips grow a mind of their own, I start to rub against him, shots of pure pleasure coursing through me, making me ache even more where I want Walker most.

"Fuck, baby. You're so hot. So soft, sweet, and smooth," he rasps, as he nips my bottom lip then deepens the kiss again. *Thump. Thump. Thump.* My heart is racing, beating hard against my chest as my hips speed up, Walker's hard thick length wedged between us, my pelvis rocking against him, our breaths coming hard and fast now. We're all hands and lips, our bodies rubbing and thrusting together in our own beautiful rhythm, and I for one can feel the crest of our climax coming up on the horizon. I snake my hand between us, lifting my hips to ride his leg and sliding my fingers inside his boxers, desperate to feel the silky smooth flesh of his cock against my skin. But Walker's body stills, it's as if a bucket of cold water has been thrown over him.

"Sweetheart, as much as I *really* like where your mind is going and where *this...*" He laces his hand with mine and squeezes it gently, "...is going, and it physically hurts me to do it, we have to stop this, before we pass the point of no return."

"Oh..." I jerk my hand from his waistband, but he catches it and slowly removes his thigh from between my legs where I was riding him like a wanton woman. I quickly try to get away by rolling out of the bed. I don't know how I can escape this embarrassing situation, but I'm willing to give it a good try. Before I can get far,

Walker's arm wraps around my waist and I'm hauled back onto the bed and pinned to the mattress by his hips. I scramble, I wriggle, I try everything I can to get out from underneath him, but he gently presses my arms above my head and lowers his head until his face is all I can see.

"Stop, baby. You're taking this the wrong way."

"How else should I take it? We were going from the good stuff to *really* good stuff. I know you're worried about going too far, but surely we can just *touch* each other without going all the way. The books say it's actual intercourse that bonds us completely. I don't understand why you keep saying we have to stop every time it starts getting good," I say, my voice getting high pitched and louder, my sexual frustration coming off as neurosis. "If it's not me, then it's because you *want* to stop. *Is it me?* Do you not want me the way I want you? If that's the case, then I'm not the One the mountain called to you. So stopping doesn't even matter. But if I am your One—and I think I am—then enjoying each other's bodies without intercourse is a perfectly viable solution to my lady boner and your rather large man boner. I'm a journalist. I look at facts and come up with conclus—" Then I can't say anything else because Walker slams his mouth down on mine, all rational thought and argument escaping me as I moan and groan and whimper and pant, my entire body jumping right back on board the *really good stuff* train as he kisses the life out of me, his tongue rough and demanding with each measured stroke.

When he finally tears his mouth away and buries his face in my neck, he lets my wrists go. I'm crawling out of my skin. I've never been so turned on before, and the things he's doing with his mouth against my throat are *not* helping.

"Um ok, I won't um..god that feels good...I won't move if you stop...um...doing that...cause it's not helping me *not* want to jump you..." Walker's mouth freezes mid-open-mouthed kiss on my neck. Slowly, he lifts his head until his amused gaze meets mine.

"At least I now know *one* way to stop you from running away," he says, his wet lips quirking up into a sexy smirk.

I narrow my eyes. "Giving me a too sexy for your own good grin like that *also* doesn't help."

He dips his chin. "Duly noted, sweetheart. Now, will you let me tell you why I had to stop when it's the absolute *last* thing I want to do—if you can't tell that already." He punctuates with a roll of his hips against mine, making my eyes flutter again.

"OK," I breathe, making his smile widen even more.

"God, you're so damn cute. It's a miracle I can think straight right now."

"What with all the blood pooling south and all that," I retort. *If he can tease me, I can tease right back.*

"Cheeky." Walker shakes his head and brushes his lips against mine. "I like you, Faith. I *really* fucking like you. There's no doubt in my mind that you're the woman the mountain has called to me. But I want to get to know you *before* we start getting caught up in making each other feel good." He grinds his hips again, and I wish he'd just take me already, but at the same time, I'm honored and awed by his restraint. Most men wouldn't hold back like this. Not when the woman lying beneath them is practically begging.

"And how to propose we do that? I feel like I know you pretty well already." I giggle as I move beneath him, brushing against his hardness and causing him to moan.

He takes another slow, gentle kiss from me before he shifts his hips away from my body. I almost pout, but then he says, "I'm going to take you outside the homestead. I want to show you *my* mountain, get you to experience why I love living here."

My breath catches and my entire body melts, any lasting pent up tension dissipating at his sweet words. I lift my hand to cradle his jaw. "I'd love that, Walker."

"Good, sweetheart. I know our time together might be short, but I really want to leave a lasting impression on you so you might wanna come back and visit *real* soon."

The world could end right now, and even that couldn't wipe the smile off my face. "Oh, I'm planning on it. And maybe you could come see me too?" Walker's face sobers slightly before he nods and kisses me, not letting up for air until my brain is fuzzy and I can barely remember the reasons why we ever have to leave this bed.

"Hope you're up for an adventure with me today, sweetheart?" he says, jumping up off the bed, and holding out his hand for mine. "Because we've gotta get a move on and get a few things from the Gear Shed before we leave."

I frown. "Gear Shed?"

"It's where we keep all the equipment for the homestead. There's the Gear Shed, then the Store Shed for non-food supplies, Green Shed for gardening, crops, and farming supplies, and a huge pantry at The Den for the food stores."

"I can just go back to my cabin and get ready while you're gone and meet you back here if it's easier?"

"*Or*," he says, wrapping his arms around my waist and drawing me in tight against him. "You do that, and I'll meet you at your cabin with my truck in about thirty minutes, then we'll hit the road."

"You gonna tell me where we're going?"

Walker shakes his head. "Nuh-uh. It's a surprise, but wear something casual and comfortable and you'll be set for Walker's big day out."

I frown, jutting my lip out into a pout. "Why can't it be Walker and Faith's Big Adventure. It has a *much* better ring to it."

"Whatever you want, sweetheart. Your wish is my command."

I throw my head back and laugh. "You're gonna regret saying that to me."

He presses his lips to mine, staring me deep in the eyes. "Something tells me nothing I do with you will ever be a regret. We're building memories, Faith. One minute, one hour, one day at a time. It's up to us to make the most of it."

8

WALKER

The minute my truck pulls into the mountain road heading toward Kenshaw, Faith turns in her seat to face me. "Are you going to tell me where we're going? You're being very mysterious."

I grab her hand and lift her knuckles to my lips. "It's a surprise."

She pulls her arm free and crosses it over her chest, drawing my attention to her breasts. *Damn, I'm a lucky man.* The mountain called my dream woman to me. She's gorgeous, smart, a firecracker with a quick wit and fantastic sense of humor, and she looks fucking amazing whether she wears a gorgeous maid of honor dress or a hoodie and sweats, better still when she's in one of my tees and her underwear like she was in my bed this morning.

Thirty minutes later, we're reaching the edge of our land at the foot of Bear Mountain. Slowing down, I bring the truck to a stop next to the Kenshaw Valley river that runs between Bear and Moose Mountains.

"If you think I'm going swimming in a mountain river after a snowfall, you've got another thing coming, mister," she says, leaning forward in her seat and looking out the windshield with wonder-filled eyes. The scenery here is beautiful. Not as beautiful as Faith but, there's only a light smattering of snow coating the ground and trees, so there's still a lot of green showing through. The river rushes past us, the melting ice from the storm fueling its urgency providing the bass line to nature's symphony. We have the sun peeking through the canopy to warm us, and the company of each other to keep us entertained.

"No swimming. But I'm gonna saving that idea for when it's summer, so I get to see you wear a bikini." I wink at her before hopping down and shutting my door behind me, moving around to help her out before leading her to the back of the truck and opening the tailgate.

"So if we're not swimming. Are we going hiking along the river? Because I love hiking. I try to find new trails to go on almost every weekend." She looks back toward the river, studying it a bit more closely this time. I chuckle and shake my head, reaching under the canopy and pulling out the fishing waders I grabbed from the equipment shed while she was getting ready.

Her eyes widen and I hold my breath, wondering if I'm completely screwed this up. Then her face splits into a huge smile when I pull out the fishing poles, and I exhale in relief. "Oh, my god. We're going fishing. Really?" She jumps into my arms and kisses me like she means it, my hands drop the gear to catch her ass so she doesn't fall.

"I used to go fishing with my dad back in Kinleyville. It's one of my favorite childhood memories. He taught me to bait the hook and everything. How did you know?" she cries, her eyes wet with happy tears.

"I didn't. This is just what I like to do when I need time to myself. Just me and the river—and hopefully at this time of year, we'll catch ourselves a nice fat rainbow trout or a coho salmon."

"For real? I'm just...this is the best surprise, Walker," she says, giving me a soft, gentle, meaning-filled touch of the lips this time. "Thank you, baby."

Fuck. I'm so far gone for this girl. She can call me baby and I'll do anything she damn well asks of me.

"We're making memories, sweetheart. Now," I say, easing her back onto her feet. "You ready to catch some fish?"

"Hell yeah, let's do it," she says, reaching for the waders. *That's my girl.* I was half expecting her to balk at the idea of wading in the river to troll for fish, but she's not only eager to join me, but she's experienced too. If ever there was a doubt, there definitely isn't one now.

Once we get set up and in the water, the fish start biting almost as soon as we drop a line in. We got spooled a couple of times when the fish took off faster than we could react, and we even got a broken line and lost an attractor on a monster trout that fought us a little too hard, but mostly, we had a lot of laughs and a lot of fun. Fishing to me is normally a solitary activity, but doing it with Faith has brought it to a whole new level.

"You think that's enough to feed everyone?" Faith gasps as she heaves a salmon into the fish box with the others. I love that she's thinking about the Homestead like that. She seems to understand that taking care of each other is our way of life and is happily embracing it.

I do a quick count of the splashing fins. "With some to spare," I say before I look up at the sky. "And if we're quick, we should be able to trade the extras for a few luxuries at the market."

"You do that?"

"Trade fish?" I ask, helping her back up onto the bank.

"Yeah."

"We trade lots of things. Whenever we have excess, we go into Kenshaw to their whole food market and we exchange our extra produce for things we can't grow ourselves. Sometimes we sell it and use that money to buy supplies from Kinleyville—"

"Which is how Serena found her way here."

"That's right. And you. For which I am eternally grateful," I say, sliding my arm around her waist and pulling her to me. Just as I slant my mouth over hers, she freezes. Her spine going ramrod straight as her fingers curl against my shirt.

"There's a b-b-bear," she whimpers, her eyes cutting to the other side of the river where a low growl emanates as a bear I've seen many times before dips her paw in the water looking for a feed.

"She's nothing to worry about. It's just Daisy. She's a pet to one of the Coopers."

"They have a pet *bear?*" Serena balks. "All I ever had was a hamster named Steve." I chuckle at the unusual name choice for a young girl.

"They sure do. The sheriff of Woodward Valley, Boone, keeps her at his home. Speaking of…" I spot the sheriff breaking through the treeline and hold my hand up in greeting. "Haven't seen you patrolling the river for a while," I call out to him.

"Oh, hey!" he says, pausing by Daisy and giving her side a good scratch. "I heard some homesteaders were out here stealing all the fish, so I thought I'd come check it out. Looks like I was right." He smiles as he says it, and I know he's teasing, but Faith doesn't take it that way.

"Are we *stealing*?" she asks under her breath.

"No, sweetheart." I laugh. "Boone here is just yanking your chain. We've got all the necessary permits, and he knows it."

"He's right. Sorry to freak you out, miss," Boone says, tipping his hat in greeting. "Say, didn't I see you at Brady and Serena's wedding last night? You were the maid of honor, am I right?"

Faith smiles. "You are. And I apologize for not being more friendly, but my time is very limited with this one here."

"Heard the call, huh? I remember what that was like. My wife, Amy came to town for a reader's retreat and never left. Well, she *tried* to leave, but I threatened to arrest her, and the rest is history. Hope you two love-birds have a smooth ride to your...what do they call it in Aster's books? Oh yeah, your happily ever after."

"Thanks, Boone. We're doing our best," I say, giving him a wave as he heads back into the forest and once again leaves us alone.

"He seems nice," Faith says, tilting her face up to me once more. "But I believe he interrupted something."

Grinning, I thread my fingers on either side of her hair and bring my mouth down on hers, kissing her until we hear the thud of an escaping salmon jumping from the box. "We should get these fish loaded up or we won't have any dinner," I say, regretfully stepping away from her. Although, I think I could happily feast on her for the rest of my life and never go a day hungry. Hopefully, we won't have to wait too long for our own happily ever after

9

FAITH

Sunday afternoon after returning to the homestead, Walker kisses me goodbye on my cabin doorstep, promising to get done with his work quickly so we can continue our day of making memories and spending time together.

And while he's doing that, I sneak in a couple of hours of work and submit my Mabel Jenkins story to buttmunch and outline another article that's due a few days after I return to Anchorage. Then it's time to visit the new Mrs. Brady Long who I've severely neglected since she said 'I do' yesterday.

When Serena answers the door, her expression can only be described as blissful. And tired. Which tells me all I need to know about her wedding night.

"Hello, Mrs. Long," I say with a smile, stepping inside and pulling her in for a huge hug.

She giggles. "God, I love the sound of that, but I'm still not used to it." She leads me into her living room, the space still a mess after all of our pre-wedding preparations yesterday. "Sorry about all the clutter. I've been otherwise occupied."

I shoot her a salacious grin, looking her up and down and pointing to the barely there bite mark on her neck. "I bet. Especially with that hickey you've got there." Serena blushes bright red, her hand darting up to cover the mark in question, a wry smile curving her lips. I hold my hands up. "Hey. My bestie had an amazing wedding night with her new husband, as she should."

Her eyes glaze over. "Yeah. It was truly magical."

"Kinda makes sense, you know, living on this magic mountain and all." We both sit on her sofa, curling our legs up and settling in.

"*Speaking* of the mountain." She narrows her eyes. "You and Walker. Spill. Because there's no way you can make goo-goo eyes at my brother-in-law throughout the wedding and dance all night with him at the reception, *and* disappear down the mountain with him this morning and tell me that nothing is going on there."

My lips twitch as I try—and fail—to hold in my salacious smirk. "Um..."

Her entire face lights up. "You're smitten, aren't you!"

My answering smile is so big that my cheeks hurt. “Yeah, I think I am.” Then I sober and reach out for her hand. “But I’m a terrible friend. I’ve been busy working and spending time with Walker, and I haven’t been here for you, which was the entire reason I came here.”

“*Or*...I may have been the catalyst, but the mountain called you here for *him.* We’ve had a lifetime of friendship and we’ll continue to have it until the day we die, but you’re totally being the bestest friend ever by making our pinky promise to marry brothers come true!”

I gasp. “We’ve just met, Rena. It’s *far* too soon to be talking about *marriage.*” My heart starts thumping in my chest, but it’s not panic I'm feeling...I think it’s *hope.*

“Pffft. I came to the homestead to make a supply delivery and look at me now,” she says, waving her heavily adorned ring finger my way.

“I *really* like him,” I whisper.

Serena’s face goes soft and gentle. “He’s a great guy, Faith. Honestly, everyone in the homestead is amazing, but Walker feels things deeper, takes things more to heart, and works that little bit harder. He never stops trying to do better...*be* better. I admire him a lot, and I honestly think he’s too hard on himself.”

“I think he’s pretty damn amazing already. I'm not even sure *how* he could be any better.” *Note to self: Make sure Walker always knows how outstanding you think he is.*

"Aww, look at you being all gushy and stuff," she says. "This is awesome. We could be sisters!"

"We're already sisters."

Serena beams. "Yeah, we are. But I'm talking legally. That'll be pretty special because our kids will be cousins." She releases a happy smile before she shakes off her daydream and focuses back on me. "Now, tell me everything," she says, leaning forward. "I want to know how serious this has become."

That's when I launch into my story about finding him naked in his cabin when I got the directions wrong, which makes her laugh uncontrollably, then our late-night dance in my living room, our night, and morning together where we *didn't* do anything that I really *really* want to do, and I finish with salmon fishing and our time at the Kenshaw Markets where I got to watch Walker haggle like a pro and come out with some amazing treats for the homestead—chocolate, honey, and nuts, just to name a few.

Serena sits back, a pleased-as-punch look on her face. "See, what did I tell you. We're totally going to be sisters," she says, leaning into me as we both dissolve into a girly fit of giggles.

"So what is the plan for tonight then?" she asks once we've calmed down, and she's fetched us a glass of wine each. Apparently, potential future sisterdom calls for celebration, who knew?

“Walker’s taking me for a picnic up at the sacred spring since the weather has lifted.” She bites her lip and looks deep in thought as she takes a long sip from her glass. “What? I know that look. You’re trying to decide whether to say something.”

Serena sighs and cradles the wine in her hands. “OK. So I’m going to impart some wisdom that I learned the hard way. Hell, *everyone* before me has learned the hard way.”

“About what? Has he got a third nipple or something? Is it hereditary and they all have it? What?”

Her lips twitch as she shakes her head. “No! It’s just... I’m going to say something as your best friend, OK?”

“OK...” I say, my brows bunching together.

“Don’t sleep together. Not yet. Not until you know you can be together and more importantly, *stay* together.”

“I know. I read Aster’s books when you gave them to me, and Walker said something similar last night.”

“That's good,” she says, breathing a sigh of relief. “Honestly. I don’t think I ever told you just how painful it was to be apart from Brady. But it *hurt*. Like, really hurt. I could barely concentrate on anything. I felt like I was a shell of myself, nervous and anxious all the time. It was so weird, and it’s not until I saw him again and knew I was here to stay for good, that the pain went away.”

"So it *is* just like in Aster's books?"

She nods. "Yep. It's the weirdest feeling in the world, and believe me, I know it's going to take a *whole* lot of restraint because this mountain"—she waves her hand in the air—"and *these* mountain men, make it *oh* so very hard."

"That they do..." I murmur, bringing my glass to my lips to take a sip to hide my smirk, a snicker escaping when Rena's mouth drops open.

"Oh, my god! Have you done it already?"

"No... just... made out a bit..."

"And..." she says, giving me a sharp look.

"Honestly, nothing else. But I wanted to." *God, do I want to.*

"So you're still leaving tomorrow then?"

I nod. "I have to. Buttmunch is expecting me back in the office first thing Tuesday morning."

"And then? What are you and Walker going to do? These men don't do well away from this mountain, I told you how it was with Brady."

I shrug. "I'll just have to visit a lot. I can work from anywhere with an internet connection, as long as—"

"As long as buttmunch lets you."

I swallow hard. "Yeah."

What I don't tell her is that after today, I've had another story idea I've pitched to buttmunch, one that might mean I won't be gone for long at all. But I want to talk to Walker about it before getting Serena's 'sisters marrying brothers' hopes up. It also might help reassure Walker how much I'm into him, because I am. I'm well and truly falling for that man already. And it should scare me, but it doesn't. *Maybe this mountain's magic is rubbing off on me too.*

Serena reaches over and squeezes my hand, locking her hopeful eyes with mine. "Have faith, Faith." She giggles. "These Bear Mountain men make it worth it, babe, I promise. If you take a chance on Walker, he'll never give you a reason to regret it."

"I want to take a chance on him more than anything. But I also love being a reporter. So work is my biggest obstacle. I'm just trying to find a way to have my cake and eat it too."

"You'll work it out, babe. You're too smart to let buttmunch derail your big HEA. And if he's got any sort of a brain in his head, he'll bend over backward to accommodate you so he doesn't lose the best darn human interest writer he's ever had."

"I hope you're right, Rena. Because I want it all—the man, the job, the *life.* Now...I just have to fight for it."

"That a girl," Serena says with a nod as she drains her glass and sets it on the table, her eyes going wide when we hear the sound of footsteps outside. "Brady's back." Her whispered words tell me that's my cue to leave. But before I do, I take one last look around the cabin, and one last look at my best friend greeting her wonderful mountain man husband with an excited embrace. *I never knew this is what I wanted, but now I can't wait until I have it.*

10

WALKER

"Well, hey there, pretty lady," I say to Patty Cooper through the serving window in The Den's kitchen. She's Gandalf's sister and mother to Martie, and came to live on the homestead when Martie and Van were still finding their way to each other. After bringing the fish in earlier, I asked if she'd be willing to set some aside for tonight so I could take Faith up to the sacred spring for a picnic dinner. Ever since Faith mentioned swimming this morning, it's all I can think about. "I hear you've got a little something special for me."

"I'm spoken for, Walker Long," she says, feigning indignation. "I'm also old enough to be your mother, *and* I'm married. Shame on you."

I chuckle at her dramatics as I stick my head through the window and sniff the air. "I don't know how any man can stay away from a woman who can cook as well as you, Patty. That fish I brought you smells like a meal."

"One that I'm almost finished preparing for you and the lovely Faith. Things are going well between you two?" She flashes me a smile as she gives a massive pot filled with baby potatoes a stir.

"The mountain chose well," I say, unable to hold back on my smile. "Now I just have to romance her well enough that she decides to let me keep her. She's leaving tomorrow and I want to give her a night to remember."

"I'm sure she'll love anything you have planned, dear. Why don't you give me about fifteen minutes to finish up and then I'll get your picnic basket to you? Actually, you can make yourself useful by going down to the cellar and picking a pinot noir or a chardonnay to go with this. Then you can romance your girl the right way so she'll never want to be away from you." She gives me a wink before turning back to her work.

With a quick thank you, I head out of The Den and into the administration building to get the keys for the cellar. Huxley and Micah work their day jobs from in here, but it's also where we manage all the back of house tasks that a community like ours requires. The Bear Mountain Homestead isn't all just about farming the land. We've got a whole host of people working to turn all the cogs that keep us running like a well-oiled machine. We have to keep track of finances, maintenance and work schedules, inventory, animal health, and purchasing. And the bigger we grow as a community, the more paperwork there is to go with it. "You're looking happy today, Mr. Smiley Pants," I say, walking in to find Nash staring at a computer with a massive frown screwing up his face.

"I can't make sense of these stupid spreadsheets," he growls. "Whose dumb idea was it to put me in charge of the work schedule? And why can't I just write it on paper like we used to."

"Because we're trying to be as paperless as possible," I say, pulling the drawer open and signing the key to the cellar out.

Nash tears his eyes from the screen and turns his glower my way. "What do you need that for?"

"Getting some wine for tonight. Taking Faith up to the spring for a picnic and a swim." I say it like it's no big deal but Nash sits back, crossing his arms behind his head and letting out a low whistle.

"Things are getting serious, my man. Good for you."

I offer him a half-grin. "Thanks, bro. I'm...happy. You know?"

"Yeah, man. I see it in you, and I'm glad it's working out. But, do me a favor, Walk?"

I close up the drawer and pocket the key as I meet his gaze. "Yeah?"

"Grab a bottle of something for me too. I'm gonna need a stiff drink if I'm ever gonna figure this new program out."

"Sure. No problem," I say with a chuckle as I head back outside to the cellar and get what I need. By the time I've taken Nash his bourbon and returned to The Den with the wine, Patty has the picnic basket ready for me.

"I put something extra special in there too," she says as she hands it to me. "Something for dessert."

"Thanks, Patty. You're a treasure. Just know, if I was an older man and you were a younger woman…"

"Oh, pfft. Off with you, you cheeky thing," she says with a laugh. I give her a chaste kiss on the cheek, then head straight for the door. I'm on my way to Faith's cabin when I find her walking in the opposite direction, obviously returning from visiting with Serena. "Perfect timing," I say, pausing until she catches up with me. I lower my head and press my lips to hers, tasting the sweetness of wine on her breath. "Started without me, huh?"

"Not really. Just a tiny tipple with my bestie. We were celebrating the day God made mountain men for us to lust after." She places her hand against my chest and leans in close.

"As long as I'm the *only* mountain man on your lust list, that's just fine with me."

"You most definitely are," she says with a hint of naughtiness in her eyes that turns me on no end. "If we don't count fictional ones, anyway."

"Ready for our picnic? I just picked the basket up from Patty, so if we hurry it'll still be piping hot."

"Give me two seconds to grab my beanie, and I'll be right with you," she says, jogging toward her cabin and letting herself inside. I could probably walk next to her just as fast as she's jogging, but it's nice to stand back and enjoy the view of her yoga-pant-wearing ass.

The moment she's back with me, with a beanie and a chunky snow jacket, I head to the small shed next to my cabin where I keep my newest toy—an electric snowmobile.

"No hiking today?"

"I figure we've done enough walking and stuff today. And besides, it means I get to have your body plastered against mine up and down the mountain."

Her eyes flash with heat. "Now *that* might be the best idea you've had so far."

"Glad you approve, sweetheart."

Although the snowmobile gets us up to the spring quicker than walking, we still have a five-minute trek to the mountaintop. While we walk, Faith talks about the article she's been working on all afternoon and how happy and in love her friend seems, and I listen carefully, loving each word that pours from her lips.

"I feel like I've been doing all the talking and you haven't managed to say a thing," she says as we step over the rocks at the entrance of the spring. I hold her hand to keep her steady.

"I've been happy hearing you talk. I like that you're so excited about your story. You sound very dedicated to your craft."

"I try. It's not hard when your boss likes to feed you the most boring stories out there. But I like to put my spin on things. And the readers seem to like them. Like my last story about a 100-year-old lady who still volunteers twice a week. She had the most hilarious stories too. She says an Applejack a day keeps the doctor away."

I bark out a laugh. "Not sure that's how the saying goes."

Faith shrugs, a smile tugging at her perfectly plump lips. "She's 100. I kind of like that she lives to the beat of her own drum."

"Or drink, so it seems."

"Exactly!" We fall silent but I keep thinking about what she said about being given the worst assignments.

"Maybe your boss gives you these stories because you're the only one capable of making them shine?" I suggest as we spread the blanket out on the lush grass then remove our snow gear as the heat from the spring presses in on us. There isn't a hint of the storm that brought snow into this area the night before last. The clearing is as untouched as ever, the only sounds we hear are the gentle bubbling of the spring and tweet of birds in the trees.

"I'd like to think that too. But I have a feeling Serena is right, and he's just a buttmunch."

I chuckle, kneeling on the rug before I open up the picnic basket, finding containers with grilled salmon, green beans with cherry vinaigrette and almonds and boiled baby potatoes with homestead-grown garlic, home-churned butter, and hydroponic parsley, along with chocolate lava cakes and cream for dessert.

"Oh, my god. That smells divine," Faith says as her stomach growls audibly. "My stomach thinks so too." She laughs as she places her hand against it.

"Patty outdid herself this time," I say, salivating over the delicious food while I pull out our plates and discover some candles tucked in there too. "She's even packed some ambiance for us."

"What could be better than this place though?" she says, looking around. "It's so spectacular. It's like a pocket world tucked away from everything else. No technology, no distractions. Just the best kind of company and a peace I can't even begin to describe."

“That’s the mountain spirit,” I explain, setting her food on her plate before handing it to her.

“Really?” She lifts her eyes in wonder as she balances her plate on her knee. “I felt it yesterday at the ceremony, but I kind of thought it was just me getting caught up in the romance. You know, chicks and weddings.”

Shaking my head slowly, I take a deep breath and let the calming energy of the spirit fill my lungs and drift throughout my body. “This is where we all come when we need time to reflect or to find guidance. No matter what is going on in your life, you can always count on leaving this place with clarity as to what your next step will be.”

“And what is it telling you to do now?” she whispers, biting the end of a green bean and chewing slowly as her eyes lock with mine.

“It’s telling me to do things we’re not ready for. It wants me to keep you.”

“You hear that?” She sucks in a breath as she looks around some more, her gaze widening.

“Not really hear...it’s more something you feel,” I say, placing my hand over my heart. “It takes a bit of practice, but if you close your eyes and concentrate, you'll feel it too.”

Setting her plate on the ground beside her, she mimics my pose, placing her hand over her heart and closing her eyes, breathing in and out slowly.

"Do you hear something?" I whisper, leaning in so my mouth is right up close to her ear.

"Yes," she responds before she opens her eyes and turns to face me, her nose brushing against mine as she places her hand against the rough stubble of my cheek. "And I think..." she pauses and swallows hard before her eyes lift to mine. "I think we should get out of those too-warm clothes and go swimming in the spring."

"What about dinner?" I ask, gently sucking on her lips.

"I'm not hungry for food." Her words come out in a whisper as she pulls away from me and gets to her feet, making a show of peeling off her clothes, one item at a time as she makes her way to the edge of the spring. She hooks her fingers on either side of her underwear, then throws a coquettish look over her shoulder before pushing them to the ground.

I let out a groan, my cock jumping at the sight of her slit peeking between her thighs before she straightens. If I get up right now, there's a chance I might trip over my dick or faint from a lack of blood to the head. *Holy hell, this woman will be the death of me.*

"Coming in?" she asks, lowering herself into the water until her luscious body is hidden from sight. *Come.*

That's about all I want to do right now. Just the vision of her in the spring with steam billowing into the surrounding air is an image that will forever be burned into my brain.

With grunts and groans the only sounds I'm capable of, I pull my shoes from my feet and nearly rip my shirt from my body as I rise to my feet, unbuttoning my pants and pushing them to the ground, boxers and all so I'm closing the distance between us completely naked.

Her eyes travel over my body and linger on my rock hard cock. It bounces as I move, tall and thick and desperate for her touch. We won't be consummating this thing between us tonight, but I plan on enjoying everything but, because we both need some sweet relief before she's forced to leave the mountain tomorrow.

"See something you like?" I ask as I lower myself onto the edge of the spring, my legs in the water and the rest of me seated on the rocks as the heat of the water rises around us and clings to my skin.

"Well, I don't see a third nipple, so that's reassuring," she teases. She wades closer to me and places her hands on my thick thighs. The touch of her wet skin on mine making me shudder in anticipation.

"Dealt with many third nipples in your time?" I ask, laughing at the unexpected comment.

"No. But it never hurts to check." Licking her lips, she lifts her eyes to mine then lowers them back to my crotch as her fingers tentatively touch the length of my cock. "Is this OK?" she asks, lifting her gaze to mine again.

I suck in a breath, my cock twitching in response as if it's arching into her touch. "It's more than OK, sweetheart. We can play all you want."

"As long as playing is all we do, right? No P in V?" She smirks as she wraps her hand around my shaft, turning my amused snort into a hissing moan.

"God, I love it when you touch me, Faith."

"What about when I...kiss you?" she asks. "Should I kiss you here?" While her hand massages my shaft, she presses her lips to the space just below my jawline. "Or should I kiss you here?" She presses a kiss to my pec, sliding her tongue over my skin. "Or should I kiss you...lower?"

I let out a groan as she presses a gentle kiss to the tip of my cock, her tongue darting out to lick the saltiness from the tip before she parts her lips and draws me into her mouth. She strokes her hand up to meet her mouth in a slow and measured dance, humming against my skin and swallowing me down deep until her lips kiss my root and my mind explodes.

"What the actual fuck is happening," I hiss, my hands going into her hair as my balls draw up tight and I have to do mathematical equations in my head so I don't embarrass myself by coming too early.

I gulp in much-needed air to try to keep calm, but then Faith looks up at me with those big baby blues and picks up the pace, and then I'm a goner. "Sweetheart, I'm going to come," I rasp out, not wanting to come in her mouth without warning, especially when I don't have the greatest control over my body right now. Her head bobs and her lips tighten but she doesn't ease up, if anything, she doubles down. Then it hits me and my fingers flex in her hair as my balls unload and I spill myself into her mouth in a thick hot rush that she seems to happily gulp down. She slowly pulls back until she's just licking my tip to make sure she has every drop.

"Yummy," she says, licking her lips as she looks up at me with those innocent eyes of hers.

"You're a devil," I say, grinning as I slide into the water and bring my mouth to hers, kissing her until my dick is twitching and ready again. I slide my hands all over her body, kissing her neck, and her breasts until I take hold of her waist and hoist her out of the water, setting her down right where I was sitting before. "Lie back, sweetheart. It's my turn."

11

FAITH

I lean back and brace my elbows on the soft ground next to the spring, my hips sit high on a rock as I spread my legs wide, exposing my sex to Walker's ravenous gaze.

Flattening his palms against the insides of my knees, he slowly glides them along my sensitive inner thighs and with his eyes locked with mine, dips his mouth to my apex and drags his tongue through my folds. My back arches at the first touch, the exquisite pleasure shooting through me as he wraps his lips around my clit, the swollen bundle of nerves throbbing with need. My muscles shake as he lifts my legs around my shoulder and blows warm air over my wet seam. Using his fingers to hold me open to him, he winks at me then dives right in, using his tongue, lips, teeth, and fingers.

I feel everything he's doing to me *everywhere* and I'm clawing out of my skin. I was already halfway to orgasm just from tasting Walker on my tongue, but now that he's eating me with renewed hunger, our groans and moans filling the air, my hips rolling up against his face, chasing the climax that coils tight inside me, wanting the come under his tongue more than I want my next breath. I swear the high altitude and sacred spring are making this entire experience more powerful, more overwhelming and surreal, but more than anything, I know the intensity between us is simply because it's Walker.

His finger toys with my entrance. "Yes. Please, baby. I want to feel you inside me," I whimper.

"Fuck yes, sweetheart." He lifts his eyes to meet my hooded, undoubtedly wild ones. I'm straddling the edge of a climax that might just break me apart, but I'm so close, I need it. I need more. I need Walker to make me soar.

Ever so slowly, he presses one finger, then two inside me, my body clenching around him, sucking him deeper, as if wanting to keep him there forever. I cry out, my body no longer under my control, I'm simply a slave to the pleasure Walker is giving me. And in my list-fueled haze, the sounds and words coming out of my mouth are unintelligible.

"Yes, baby. Let me hear you. Fuck," he rasps, swirling the tip of his younger around my clit before nipping my sex. “I could live between your legs, with your taste on my tongue. So damn sweet.” My shoulders drop back to the ground, my hands gripping his head and holding him to me, my toes curling as my legs tingle, my muscles growing tighter and tighter like a coiled spring being wound so taut, the energy building up like a cresting wave ready to—

“Come for me, sweetheart,” Walker growls as he buries his fingers deep and takes his teeth against my clit, drawing it hard between his lips. I detonate, my torso lifting off the ground, my grip on Walker’s hair pulling tight as wave after wave of ecstasy contorts my body, the mind-bending orgasm sending me high into the stratosphere before Walker slows his ministrations and gently brings me back down to the land of the living.

Dragging his lips up my body, Walker rises out of the water until he’s covering me, his cock hard and hot again as it presses into my soft stomach.

I tug his mouth down onto mine, delving my tongue between his lips and languidly rolling it against his. The taste of my arousal and everything that is *Walker* sends another smaller wave of lust coursing through me.

“Damn, you’re good at that,” I murmur breathlessly against his now smiling lips.

“God, I’m so glad the mountain chose you for me.”

"The feeling's mutual. Now, let's get back into the water. Something tells me I need this sacred spring to work it's magic on my muscles if we're ever gonna get back down to the cabin."

Walker eases off me and slowly guides me back below the surface, drawing me close into his arms and running his nose along mine before brushing his lips against my mouth. "Don't worry, sweetheart. I'll take care of you. And if you let me, I always will."

WE WAKE up late Monday morning, tired after our late night at the sacred spring, but also because we know that today is the day I have to leave the homestead and head back to my life in Anchorage.

My body is plastered to his side, my hand roaming his chest, touching and stroking every inch of it as I commit this moment to memory, knowing it might be awhile until we can be like this again.

"Tell me not to go," I whisper. Walker's hand that was rubbing circles on my back falters before slowly starting up again.

"Don't go." He smiles and sucks gently on my swollen lips. "Stay here forever with me."

"I want to," I groan. "But I have to go. I've got work to do and plants to water. It sounds mundane, but my life is in that city and I worked *really* hard to get where I am."

"I know, sweetheart," Walker murmurs, his voice soft and understanding. "You know I don't want you to leave, but I also know that you've got important work to do. You've got a voice that needs to be heard, stories that need to be told." I let his words wash over me, cloaking me in reassurance. He wants me to go about as much as I do—that being not at all—but to hear him have such a belief in my work and my words, I feel emboldened. I think that maybe I can stand my ground against buttmunch and his bullshit, and demand to be treated fairly for the quality of my work.

"That's what it's all about—the story. I love digging into the person behind the news and finding out more about them. Why they do what they do, what makes them unique..."

"It takes a special kind of person to be objective in that way. I suppose you have to play devil's advocate to get the real truth out of a subject. Which leads me to an idea I've been toying around with."

"What kind of idea?"

"Why don't you just tell your editor you're writing a human interest story about the homestead? You could write about the work we're doing here to protect the environment and its resources, help raise awareness about climate change and sustainability, while focusing on the human's that choose to separate themselves from the mainstream world. It'll mean you can stay right here, in my bed, in my cabin, in my arms while you write it." He rolls me over and covers my body with his before tangling his fingers in my hair and planting a hot as hell wet, deep, and *highly* convincing kiss on my lips as if backing up his suggestion with the most important reason why. When we finally break apart, we're both panting and I can see the same longing and veiled heat in his gaze that I'm feeling right now. Both of our minds are going back to the amazing night we had at the spring last night. God, I *really* need to get back here as soon as I can so we can seal the deal and claim each other once and for all.

"Why don't you just come with me?" I blurt out, verbalizing the idea as soon as it comes to mind.

His green eyes go soft. "I wish I could, sweetheart. But I can't. With Brady and Serena just married, they're going to be off the grid for a while"

"They are? Serena said they weren't going away."

"That's because she doesn't know that Brady is stealing her away for a few days to stay at a secluded cabin about an hour from here where no one can disturb them."

My eyes light up, my heart jumping with excitement. "They're *totally* gonna make a honeymoon baby," I say with a happy sigh. I'm absolutely over the moon for my bestie and her new hubby. Better yet, when Serena and Brady start popping out mountain babies, I'm claiming god mom status for every single one of them.

Walker throws his head back and laughs. "Probably. But since I'm Brady's 2IC, I'm next in line so to speak, which means I have to run things so they can have a honeymoon and Brady isn't stressing about the Homestead."

"OK. So the plan is, I'll go back to Anchorage and convince my editor to let me write a piece about how one community is trying to combat climate change, one eco-friendly homestead at a time, and then he'll just let me come right back. It's a longshot. But I'll give it all I've got."

"If he doesn't go for it, you could always come and write for the paper in Kenshaw. It's tiny, and they only hit the press once a month, but that's a possibility too." My heart swells at the belief he has in me and us. I already know that we both want to be together to see where our feelings will lead, but hearing him coming up with different options to make it a reality awes me.

A resigned sigh escapes my mouth. "You're right. *Ugh.* Why doesn't the mountain offer solutions with her call? Like a roadmap to happiness or something."

"Because you've got to work for the things you want. And we want each other, so that means we endure whatever hardship is coming our way." I melt into him, letting his words sink in as I press my forehead to his and close my eyes, just breathing him in while I can.

"I really *really* like you, Walker. You're the best thing I never saw coming," I whisper, punctuating my declaration with a soft kiss to his lips.

"Making memories, sweetheart. Remember that. That's what we're working toward. But I'm sure gonna miss your heat in my bed, your soft body against mine, and those sweet kisses I can't get enough of."

I smile as he kisses me this time, our lips still touching as we steal as much time as we can before I have to go. "I'll still save you all the dances."

His arms wrap around me and give me a squeeze. "Good. Because I'm already looking forward to the next one, right here, in my bed..." His tongue darts out and traces the seam of my mouth, making me moan. "And very much naked."

"Damn. Now I really, *really* don't want to leave." He chuckles and buries his face in my neck and sets out to make me squirm and moan a bit more before I have to go.

A few hours later, my bags are packed away in Bertha's trunk and I'm struggling to come up with another reason to delay the inevitable. I know I'll be coming back to visit, but that doesn't do anything to ease the tightness in my chest.

I turn to Serena and we wrap our arms around each other, standing there for what seems like ages as we hug tight. "I'm gonna miss you."

She laughs and steps back, resting her hands on my shoulders and meeting my eyes. "You always say that. It never matters how far away we are or how long we don't see each other, you're always my sister for life." She leans in so her mouth is by my ear. "But something tells me it won't be so long between visits next time." I huff out a breath, blinking rapidly to stave off my tears. *Ugh. Why is this so damn hard?*

"Yeah. Well, let's see what *magic* I can weave back in Anchorage so that I can come back as soon as possible."

Her grin widens. "I believe in you and I *know* you'll be back before you know it, or Walker will come to you. It's the mountain's way, after all." She winks at me before Brady steps up and draws her into his side.

"Safe travels," he says, his eyes crinkling at the sides.

I smile. "You too." That earns me a deep chuckle, I join him when Serena looks between the two of us with an adorable confused expression.

When they move back, Walker helps me into the car, his jaw clenched tight as he closes Bertha's door behind me.

Thump. Thump. Thump. My heart bangs against my chest as I turn and look up to meet his now soft, gentle gaze. I hold my breath, a lump forming in my throat as he leans down, bracing his arms on the window frame.

We stare at each other, the air between us growing so thick the tension and emotion between us is near palpable.

Then we snap, both moving at once, Walker's hands cupping my cheeks and holding me in place as he slams his mouth down on mine so hard and deep and full of feeling, I swear our lips will be bruised for days after this. But it's hands down one of the best kisses we've shared so far, because it's an unspoken promise that this will not be the last time we see each other. We've got many more memories to make, dances to share, and stories to finish.

When we finally break free, we're both breathless. "Drive safely, and call me when you get back home, OK?" he orders, his voice as rough as sandpaper. "And pitch the story to your boss. We'd love to help you with it."

I tilt my head to the side, my mouth tipping up. "You just want me to come back here as soon as possible."

He grins. "Well, *duh*. Who else will I go salmon fishing with?"

I love that grin. I want to see more of it. *Every day wouldn't be enough.*

"I'm taking a bit of the mountain spirit with me to give me good luck."

"You don't need luck, sweetheart. You've just gotta believe." He gives me one last kiss and slowly straightens. "Then you can get your sexy ass back to here where you belong."

And as I give one last wave and drive Bertha out the gates, I take a deep breath of Bear Mountain air and turn my car in the direction of home, where *hopefully* I won't be for long.

12

WALKER

"What is *this?*" Mason reaches across the desk and snatches the plans I was drawing off the table, holding them out to his twin. "He's sketching a *cabin extension*." His brows waggle up and down as Miller takes the crude design from him and scrutinizes it.

"*Three* bedrooms. Oh, brother, you have got it *bad.* She hasn't even moved here yet and you're already planning babies." Miller makes kissy noises at me as I reach out and snatch the drawing back.

"It doesn't hurt to be prepared, thank you very much," I retort, turning the plans over so they can't study them any closer. Especially since I wasn't quite finished with the drawing and there will actually be *four* bedrooms in this plan. I'd like a large family, and room to enjoy adult alone time with Faith. There's nothing wrong with that.

"Bro, we thought Brady had it bad with Serena," Mason says. "He was all growly and shit whenever they were apart and just hell to be around."

"I remember," I mutter.

"But you're like a little girl drawing love hearts with Mr. and Mrs. inside. I'm surprised you're not out there carving her name on a tree—or have you already done that?" Miller says, finishing Mason's train of thought. As the baby of the family, I'm used to the terrible twosome giving me shit, so it's like water off a duck's back with me.

"Fuck off," I say, fighting the smile that's threatening to overwhelm me. It's only been a couple of days since Faith left and I already miss her like crazy. There's an ache in my chest that I know won't go away until she's back here in my arms, but I'm optimistic over her return.

We've been calling each other multiple times a day, so I know she's already given her proposal to her editor and is waiting to hear back from him. I have a great feeling that she's going to be back here real soon, so I'm drawing up these plans as a further enticement to show her what our life will be like together. I want to give her everything she wants and needs and then some. Just like how the mountain has provided for us founding sons, I want to provide for my woman. I plan to treat her like a queen. It's how my father treated my mom and how he raised us to be. And I think Mom and Dad would've liked Faith, especially her zest for life and love of hiking and fishing. *She's totally perfect in every way.*

"Maybe we should take him down to that biker bar in town," Miller says with a snicker. "I'll bet someone there will be handy with a tattoo gun. They can put Faith's name on his ass with a cute little love heart around it."

"Oh yeah. Hell, Walk. I'll even pay for it, and I don't pay for anything."

"Bro, if I was gonna put anything on my ass, it'd be a picture of your lips kissing it after I beat you stupid for wasting your time in here when you should be out repairing the roof on cabin twelve after it lost a shingle and a raccoon got in."

Both twins make a face at me. "You're *so* not fun," one of them mutters as they leave the administration building and get back to work. The moment they're out of sight, I flip my sketch over and take a mouthful of the coffee that's gone cold beside me. I go through my to-do list, checking off everything I've done for the day. I've put through orders, balanced the books, and approved Nash's work roster, so now I can take a much-needed break, refresh my drink, and dream a little more about the life I have coming. *The mountain always provides,* I think to myself as I draw another box to represent a nursery on my plans.

"How many kids you plan on having?" Nash asks as he walks in from the kitchenette, placing a fresh mug of coffee in front of me and moving the cold one away. He's wearing his cop uniform, so he's obviously about to head down the mountain to work.

"Thanks," I say, enjoying a mouthful of *hot* caffeine goodness this time. "I keep forgetting that I make them."

"Comes with the territory, I guess. There's a lot to do when you're the man in charge."

"It's not so bad. I like keeping busy."

"You didn't answer my question," he says, tapping the paper I've been sketching on.

"Oh, I don't know. At least three. More, if that's what Faith wants. But the mountain will guide us."

"I love how sure you are about all this." He sits on the edge of my desk as he slurps from his mug. "I mean, I meant what I said at the wedding. I'm not one hundred percent sure I believe in leaving it up to the mountain to choose my soulmate. But I do enjoy seeing my brothers happy."

His words make me smile because I know without a doubt that he's going to be next. The mountain spirit loves a challenge, and a skeptical founding son will certainly provide that for her. But when it happens, he's going to be gob smacked over how sure he is about the woman meant to be his. "You'll see, brother. I have a sneaking suspicion you might find out sooner than you think."

"Why? Have you been talking to Gandalf?" He crosses his arms over his chest and narrows his eyes. It's his quintessential cop pose, funnily enough, Boone has the same stance too.

"I thought you didn't believe in the call?" I smile as I tuck my sketch away so I can get back to work. The homestead doesn't run itself, that's part of the beauty of the place besides the mountain, the community, and living our lives alongside our brothers.

"Who doesn't believe in the call?" Gandalf says, picking the perfect moment to walk in with his trusty leather book in hand.

"No one," Nash says, backpedaling quickly.

"Nash doesn't," I say at the same time, grinning wildly as Gandalf pulls his snowy-haired head back in surprise.

"But you're a founding son," he blusters, unwinding the cord from his book and flipping through the pages. "And it seems that your One will be here quite soon. Three moons, maybe? An artist or a creator if I'm not wrong." He lifts his eyes from the aging pages of his little book of prophecies and frowns at Nash. "Will you turn her away just because you don't want to believe?"

“No. I…” Nash looks from Gandalf to me, that brash exterior of his giving way to panic. It’s easy to deny something you’ve never experienced before, another to look a gift horse completely in the mouth. “I guess we’ll just see what happens, won’t we? If this call is as powerful as you all say it is. I won't be able to resist, will I? Then I guess I'll just eat my words. Will that make you happy?”

Gandalf and I look at each other before turning back to Nash. “Yes,” we say in unison.

“I need to get to work,” Nash grumbles, placing his half-drunk coffee on my desk and backing out of the office before we can make him any more uncomfortable.

“An artist you say?” I look at Gandalf and he nods.

“That's what the mountains tell me.”

“Maybe we can get her to make a new Bear Mountain Logo or something? Reckon we could do with a nice big sign over the entryway to welcome newcomers.”

“You know, I think that might be just the thing,” Gandalf says, opening his book and scratching something inside. “I’ll put a want ad in the Kenshaw Gazette?”

“Yes! That’s exactly what we need. And send the applicants to me. I’ll make sure Nash is the one who has to interview them.”

"Brilliant! I know you have a bit of a chip on your shoulder about not being seen as a leader in the homestead. But I have to tell you, Walker, you do a fine job every single day. You've grown into a well-rounded, resourceful man, and I'm glad the mountain has chosen to reward you and the lovely Faith."

"Thank you, Tim," I say, deciding to use his real name after paying me such a nice compliment. "That means a lot."

Gandalf nods my way before exiting the building, leaving me to my work and daydreaming as I count down the moments until Faith calls. I have a feeling she'll have good news for me today.

13

FAITH

"Faith, can you swing by my office before you go?" Buttmunch calls out from his office as I walk past his door.

"Sure. I just need to shut down and pack up."

"OK. No rush." My step falters at Marvin's sudden change in disposition. He's usually gruff, aloof, downright rude, indifferent, bored, or all of the above. Yet this is the third time today where he's spoken to me like I'm a human being. It's disconcerting.

Tuesday morning, I pitched my idea for the Bear Mountain Homestead story to both Buttmunch and the owner of the Anchorage Press, giving them a brief rundown of the history, the huge fan following due to Aster's two mountain man series, and then reminded them of the big news story last year where Van—who lives at the homestead—worked with the Coopers to save both Moose and Bear Mountains from development, defeating his father to protect the land he was sent to Alaska to acquire. Finally, I went in for the kill and added how much national media interest the story could potentially garner, especially with the climate change and sustainability talking points. I framed the piece as 'how one community is trying to save the world, one mountain at a time.'

Marvin looked skeptical, Giles looked like a kid at Christmas. That's when I doubled down, giving it one last shot because even after one night sleeping without Walker's arms round mine, I was missing that man like crazy. "I'll continue with my current workload while also doing interviews and researching the Bear Mountain story."

That was two days ago and now, I'm near on skipping to my shoebox of a cubicle. I'm packing up my laptop and clearing my desk when my cell pings with a notification. I'm already smiling when I open the photo message from Walker because it's a photo of him and Mason standing in the middle of the Den, posing together like they're a dancing couple. Mason taking it that one step further by holding a single red rose in his teeth.

Me: I'm jealous and pissed, Walker Long!

Walker: What? Why? I promise you're a much better dancer than my brother.

I giggle and shake my head at the phone.

Me: You were supposed to save ALL of your dances for me. I'm away from the mountain for two days and I'm already being replaced as your dance partner.

Walker: Sweetheart, the second you set foot back here at the homestead, you can dance with me whenever, wherever, and however you want.

Me: Clothes on or off?

Walker: Damn. Don't torture a man like that. I can still taste you on my tongue.

Me: Stop talking dirty when I'm still in the office. I am a good girl, remember? I'll call you when I get home.

Walker: I'll look forward to it.

I'm still smiling when I hook my messenger bag over my shoulder and walk toward Marvin's office, tapping my knuckles on his door and holding my breath as I brace myself for whatever he's about to lay on me.

Instead of a look of disdain, buttmunch actually *smiles* at me. "Come in, Faith. Take a seat," he says, waving his hand toward the chair opposite his desk.

My body jolts but thankfully I quickly school my reaction and cross the room to sit down, placing my bag on my lap.

"Did you get your stories squared away?"

I nod. "Yes, sir."

"Good. So you can head out, go home, pack your bags, and head off to the mountains."

"What?" I say on a gasp, my brows nearly touching my hairline.

His thin pencil lips twist up on one side. "Giles liked the pitch, especially the exposure opportunities for the paper, so he—we—have agreed to give you seven days to research, interview, and submit your copy to us. So by the end of business next Friday, I expect to have a completed article in my email."

"Yes, sir. Thank you. For your belief and—"

"Don't misunderstand me, Faith. I half expect you to fall flat on your face with this one, but Giles likes you and trusts you to bring your 'unique voice' to this article," he says, adding in air quotes for punctuation.

I nod, biting my tongue because there's no missing Marvin's condescending tone. I knew his niceness wouldn't last long. Moving to my feet, I make my way out the door.

"And Faith? Make sure this story has legs, because if not..." He quirks a brow, but he doesn't need to finish that sentence because I know this is my make or break moment. And I'm not just meaning in my career.

Two hours later I'm home and zipping up a second suitcase—I'm an over-packer when I want to be, sue me—and standing in the middle of my bedroom staring down at my twin bed.

I first moved into this apartment when Serena and I came from Kinleyville for college. We had big dreams and stars in our eyes; the world was our oyster. I was studying journalism, and she was doing environmental science. We were two small-town girls expanding their horizons and working hard toward vocations we were both passionate about.

But then real life hit, and in our final year, Rena gave it all up and returned to our hometown to look after her father, Titus, after he suffered a heart attack. That meant I had to buck up and put up if I wanted to stay living in this apartment and in the city I'd come to call home. So, while finishing my degree, I worked as a TA for a bit then my professor spoke to Giles, and the rest is history. And as much as buttmunch doesn't like me and the way I got my internship, he hasn't moved to get rid of me. Part of me thinks he *does* like my work, he just won't admit it.

Looking around my bedroom though, it doesn't feel the same to me anymore. *Maybe because I left my heart on the mountain with Walker.* It's no longer my warm and cozy sanctuary. It pales in comparison to the mood, the atmosphere, the sense of community, and the magic I felt at the homestead.

I may only have seven days to write this story, but part of me wonders if I should be packing everything up because it was hard to leave after three days, it might be impossible to do it after a week.

Just then, my phone vibrates on the nightstand where it's charging for the long drive.

Walker: Any word on whether the homestead story has the go-ahead yet?

My fingers hover over the keys as I toy between telling him the truth or just leaving tonight and getting there in time so Walker and I don't have to spend another night apart. *Yes, I can slide into bed next to him and surprise the hell out of him.*

Me: Hopefully tomorrow I'll have an answer for you.

Tomorrow, I'll be lying in your arms where I belong.

And as I lock my front door, load my suitcases into Bertha's trunk, and get situated behind the wheel of my beloved car, another text comes through.

Walker: If it means you will be lying here in my arms by the weekend, then the torture will be worth it.

I look up at my little apartment, wondering if I could leave my life here for one with Walker on Bear Mountain.

And with a slow-growing grin on my face, I realize that there's no question. My answer is an absolute and resounding yes.

14

WALKER

On the homestead, it's unusual to hear a car engine in the wee hours of the morning. When you do, it tends to signal some sort of problem or even an emergency. So when I'm pulled from dreamland by the squeaking of brakes and the sound of an engine cutting, I'm quick to check it out.

A momentary look out the window tells me it's an emergency of a different kind—of the heart—because my One has returned and it's Faith quietly getting out of her car, obviously hoping not to be noticed. But the loud *thump. thump. thump* of my pulse would ruin any surprise reunion she has planned. My soul knows she's back on the mountain.

"Yes!" I fist pump the air and run for the door, skipping the shoes and the coat to protect me from the cold, because I don't care about anything besides getting her back in my arms as soon as possible.

“Hey, handsome,” Faith says as she closes her car door and turns to see me approaching. “Surprise.”

“Surprise in-fucking-deed,” I rush out, stooping down to pick her up and kiss her against the side of the car. Her legs circle my hips as my mouth returns to the place it belongs—tangled up with hers. It's like the other half of my soul has returned. I've missed her like crazy this past week and my body knows it, leading the charge of this impromptu reunion. My tongue dives into her mouth, tasting her, renewing our connection—that feels as strong as it’s ever been—before I lift her from the car and walk her toward my cabin.

“My bags,” she whispers in between peppering kisses all over my lips, my jaw, and my neck.

“You won’t need them tonight,” I growl out, not stopping until we’re behind the closed door and I'm laying her down on my bed, holding myself over her and looking into her gleaming blue eyes. "I've missed you.”

“I missed you more.” She laces her fingers behind my neck and draws me in, kissing me deep and moaning into my mouth before rolling her body beneath mine. This kiss is longer, softer, and full of so much feeling I fear my heart might explode.

“You’re back.” I push up on my elbow and study her sweet face, my grin impossible to control.

“I couldn’t get here fast enough.”

Dipping my head, I kiss her some more. My hands roam her luscious body, my fingers sliding beneath her coat and pushing it off her shoulders. Then I'm running my palms under her shirt, my hands framing her ribs. She moans at my touch and I give her side a light squeeze. I can't get enough of her, I need to touch her everywhere, kiss her, *feel* her.

"And you're just rushing back home again?" I press my lips to the curve of her neck, nibbling lightly on the soft and delicate skin, desperate for more of her, wanting it all.

"No rushing this time." Her fingers glide into my hair as I shift lower, nuzzling her T-shirt covered breasts and kissing her through the fabric before helping her sit up and slowly unwrapping her like the prize she is.

The jacket is the first to go, followed by the shirt, then her bra. "You're so incredibly beautiful," I murmur, my fingers drifting over her skin with a gentle touch that leaves goosebumps in its wake, her nipples drawing tight before I lean down and take one on my mouth and hum. "So fucking sexy."

"Oh, that feels good," she whispers, dragging her nails over my bare shoulders, making me groan and my dick throb in my pants.

"You want more of that?" I move to the other side and lave my tongue around the outside of her nipple before

I drawing the bud into my mouth and sucking softly. She moans and presses into me.

"I want it all, Walker. I want you."

I gently push her onto her back and brace my body over hers. "You're all I want, sweetheart. I haven't stopped thinking about you and wishing I had you right here, naked in my bed under me."

She scrapes her nails down my chest and smiles up at me. "I hope I get a chance to be on top too."

"On top, on your side, your knees..." I kiss my way down her body, hooking my fingers in the waist of her pants and pulling them down her legs, panties and all. "Hell, I can even hang a swing from the ceiling and fuck you from there."

"Oh, you don't know how much I've been wanting to hear you say that."

I pause as I drop her pants on the floor, my eyes jerking back to hers. "The swing?"

"No, silly," she snickers as she shifts to her knees and moves down the bed. "The fucking part." She shoots me a sexy grin and wastes no time in pushing my pajama pants to the floor, both of us now naked and ready for the next important step as she wraps her hand around my aching cock. *I'm so glad she's back.*

"I've missed your touch," I say, bringing our mouths together and kissing her languidly, sliding my hand between us, finding her heat, and slipping a finger inside her. She's already so wet and hot. She feels like heaven and I can't wait to claim her as mine forever.

"I've missed yours too," she murmurs, whimpering when I add a second finger and tease her clit with my thumb at the same time. We kiss and touch each other, moaning as we draw closer to climax. "I want you inside me, Walker. Please don't say no again."

"I won't, sweetheart. This is happening. You and me. We belong together."

"We do." Slowly, she lies back on the bed and spreads her legs for me, her glistening apex beckoning me inside. I make a show of climbing up her body, kissing and licking the entire way until my gaze locks with hers and my tip is lined up with her entrance, Then I'm pushing inside, a guttural groan crossing my lips at the sensation of her exquisite heat surrounding me.

She releases a pleasure-filled gasp as I bury myself to the hilt before pulling right back until I'm almost out and sliding right back in again, picking up speed. "Heaven," I murmur.

"Walker." Her fingers bite into my skin as we move together, hips rolling, rocking, and thrusting against one another. She's slick, warm, and tight, and I'm already close, but I want to hold on and come with her. I reach between us and touch my thumb to her clit.

"I'm so in love with you, Faith," I say, driving into her, harder, faster. My voice rough and low, my body so attuned to hers now, it's like our entire beings are being meshed together as one. It feels so right, it feels like home.

"Oh god. I love you too." She tips her head back, her mouth open as moans escape her throat, short sharp gasps that match my movement and signal her impending orgasm. I know she's close to falling off the edge, so when her nails grip my skin and her core clenches tight around me, I know it's only moments away. "I'm coming!"

"Fuck. Yes." I pump my hips a few last times, our damp skin slapping together as she calls out and pulses around me. With one final thrust, I let myself go, spilling inside her and filling her with my hot seed. "Welcome home, sweetheart." I kiss her gently as I slowly stroke us back down to earth.

"What a welcome it was," she whispers, smiling against me. "But just so we're clear—how happy are you that I'm back?"

"Fucking ecstatic," I say, punctuating my answer with my hips, making my cock flex inside her.

She lets out a giggle. "Show me," she whispers, pushing my shoulder to urge me onto my back before climbing on top of me, showing *me* instead.

As the sun comes up, we're exhausted but sated, tangled up in each other's arms. I don't think I've ever felt as happy as I do at this moment. Sure, I have a full day of work ahead of me and I've barely slept a wink, but my woman is back and I'm never letting her go. My life is complete. And unlike Brady and Serena, we only had to be apart for five days—but that was far too long as it was.

"What's the plan for your first day back on the homestead?" I ask Faith as I trail my fingers up and down her naked back.

"I was hoping there'd be more of this," she says from where she's sprawled across my chest, her head on my pec, her dark hair fanned out across my shoulder. "But I'm guessing you have important boss-man things to do. So I'll probably make a start on my story."

"Your story? He said yes?" She lifts her head to meet my eyes.

"Yeah. The one about the homestead. It was your suggestion, remember? Buttmunch gave me seven *whole* days to work on it. So you've got me *all* week."

Suddenly I'm carefully setting her aside on the mattress and sitting up, pinning my wide gaze on her now cautious one. "A week? You're not staying?"

"Well...I will stay...eventually. I just...Wait. Did you think I was... and that's why we...Oh *crap.*" She shifts so she's kneeling beside me as I slump back against the headboard. "I'm sorry, Walker. I didn't think..."

"I should have asked more questions," I say, huffing out a frustrated breath and threading my fingers with hers. "I guess I wanted it to be true, so I didn't bother clarifying. But, Faith, now that we've spent the night together, you really can't be gone long. You'll need to find a way to stay on the mountain." My heart hammers against the wall of my chest. I already feel the bond between us meshing together, forming a chain that can never be broken. It's so tightly woven that I can't imagine how it would withstand any distance between us again.

"What if I work the week in Anchorage and come back here for the weekends?"

"That's not going to work. Not long term. Besides, the drive would exhaust you." I entwine my fingers with hers and brush my lips against her knuckles. "It's my job to tire you out, not the fight to see each other."

"Well, I need a job," she says sharply, her muscles tensing. "I can't just give up everything I've worked for to come here and expect you to pay my way. I need to pull my weight."

"And you will. Just like everyone else does on the homestead."

"So, I should forget about my student loans? My family? And just become a *farmer*?"

I pull my head back in surprise, sensing this conversation is heading down a dangerous road but unable to hold back. "For the record, farming is the least of what we do here. But is that such a bad thing? What, is it beneath you now?"

"What? No. It's not *beneath* me. That's not what I meant," she expels a rough breath. "I'm just not going to quit my job because I fell in love with you and the mountain. I know I'm going to end up here. I want to spend my life here with you, Walker, so please don't think I'm dissing this place or you. You are my future, OK? I've never been more sure about that. I just have to find a way to do the job I love, while also staying here and building a life with the man I love. A big step toward achieving that is proving myself with this story." She takes my hand in hers and presses a kiss to my knuckles just as I did to hers, the move soothes and helps my heart rate slow back down to its normal pace. "I know we should have waited longer to be together, Walker. But last night...it was truly magical. Even though I know it's going to hurt us to be apart after this, I'm still glad we did it. I feel so much closer now that I'm connected with you. And I promise, *I promise,* I'll find a way to stay up here permanently. The sooner, the better, because there's so much more of *that* I want to do with you."

I swing my eyes to hers, my entire body reacting as she gives me a sweet smile, then sucks my index finger into her mouth. "I don't regret it either," I murmur, finding it impossible to stay even mildly annoyed at her when all I want to do is spend the rest of our lives chained to this bed making love. "I'm sorry for being a grouch. I just hate the idea of saying goodbye to you again. You can't know how distracted I've been just wondering what you were doing and how your day was."

"Well, how about we go into town while I'm here this week and check to see if the paper has any openings? It's not a tabloid the size Anchorage Press is, but it's an option, right? If I can't get buttmunch to let me work remotely, it gives us a choice. And if all else fails, I can always go freelance."

"That sounds like a perfect compromise," I whisper, sliding my hand into her hair and pulling her in for another kiss. And as my body ignites, I realize that the chores are just going to have to wait.

15

FAITH

"Hey Patty," I say, walking into the Den. It's Sunday morning, and Walker left me sleeping—OK, *exhausted*—in bed, telling me he'd be back after the markets. Then he planted a big delicious kiss on my lips and I went back to dozing with a huge smile on my face.

But after spending yesterday making up for lost time and barely leaving our cabin, I know I have to catch up today and ask around the residents to see who I can interview, which of the founding sons I can shadow for a few hours at a time, and then I want to meet with Gandalf to talk about the history and the prophecy. The way Walker explains him, he's like a spiritual leader who can see the future—that's why they're always turning to him for guidance. He sounds fascinating, so he's a must on my list. But I know there will be other areas of interest that will pop up as I get further into this investigation. There's a lot about this place I don't yet know.

First up, I'm killing two birds with one stone by getting breakfast while talking to Patty, the mom of Marta—the mountain's prophesied queen—and also a Cooper, albeit by marriage. But her surname and the fact she's raised six children under mountain lore that makes her a great starting point.

"Hey, stranger. Fancy seeing you out of your cabin," she says with a glint in her eye. It makes me blush, an awkward giggle bubbling out of me. "Don't you be embarrassed, Faith. I remember what new love is like. I don't think Rick and I came up for air until *weeks* when we first locked eyes on each other." *Weeks? Sheesh.* "Anyway, it's far too early to be talking about that—at least when other people are around. Are you here for sustenance? I mean, food?" She gives me a wink.

"Mom, stop tormenting the poor girl when she doesn't have Serena here to run interference," Marta says, coming up beside me. "Glad to see you back, Faith. I bet Walker is happy as a crab in mud."

I can't help but grin. "Yeah, you could say that."

"Well, I'm definitely not complaining about having another female on the mountain. Us girls have to stick together, am I right?"

I nod and look between the two women. "Actually, I'm writing a story about the great work you're all doing in the homestead to protect the mountain and live a more sustainable life."

"OK. Does that mean you want to interview us?"

"If you don't mind. I don't have to use direct quotes. I'm envisaging more of an observational piece so names won't necessarily be included." I glance at Marta. "I would like to set the scene and use the thwarted development plans that Van's father had for Moose Mountain as background, as well as the spotlight Aster's books have shone on both of the mountains and the towns of Woodward Valley and Kenshaw."

"That's fine by me, I love stories that have happy endings and my darling husband and beautiful baby girl are a testament to the fact that the good guys win in the end."

"Awesome," I reply, just as my stomach growls loudly. "And I guess I'd love some breakfast. I only have six days left to submit this story, so I'm going to need all the energy I can get."

"Especially for those nighttime activities of yours," Patty says, earning a snort from me and a shake of her daughter's head. "Take a seat right here and I'll prepare a spinach, cheese, and egg white omelet for you, quick as a flash."

"Sounds amazing. Thank you. And if you can, please add me to whatever kitchen or chores roster there is. I want to immerse myself in everything homestead while I'm here."

Both women stop what they're doing, and I feel the weight of their stares bore into me. "Wait. You're *leaving*?"

"I...I have a job and an apartment back in Anchorage. I kind of have to commute in between until I can shore up remote working, freelance work, or maybe even write for the paper in Kenshaw."

Marta tilts her head and studies me, her eyes looking me up and down. "Girl, I hate to break it to you—and maybe Serena already filled you in—but once you're with your one and only, it's hell on earth to be apart from them, even when you *know* you're coming back."

"I know," I say, my voice breaking. "But my career is important to me, it's part of who I am. And I love Walker, believe me, he's my One too, I feel it whenever I even *think* about him, let alone when we're together and—"

"Incoming," Marta mutters just moments before a chorus of thumping of work boots enters the room. I turn to see Nash, Jake, and the twins coming toward us.

The twins grin at me as they move straight for the two giant industrial refrigerators lining the side of the kitchen. "Hey, Faith," they say in singsong unison, the amusement in their tone obvious.

"Hey..." I say slowly, my brows bunching together in confusion. I feel like there's a private joke I'm missing out on.

"Nice to see Walker has let you out of his sight," Nash says, walking up and kissing my cheek. My body jerks in surprise. This is Nash we're talking about. He's friendly, but he's not demonstrative. He's always rather boorish and stoic. "And ignore Tweedledum and Tweedledee, they're idiots who try to find a joke in everything and about everyone."

"OK. Good advice."

"Guys, Faith is writing an article about the homestead and what we do, the mountain, the life, the community and the like. You all okay with her taking turns to follow you around to see what you all do during the day?" Martie asks as they unscrew the lids of their aluminum water bottles and take a thirsty drink, an apple in each of their hands. *They even eat alike.*

"Damn, looks like Mason and Miller will have to *do* something for once," Nash teases, a cheeky glint in his eye.

"Screw you, Deputy."

"That's a deputy who has to go to work, thank you very much," Nash retorts before turning to me. "You're welcome to come see me Tuesday on my day off. I can show you around Kenshaw and take you to the sheriff's office if you want."

I beam up at him. "That would be awesome, Nash. Thank you."

"Oh, we can do *soooo* much better than that, can't we, Mase?" Miller says, forgetting about the fridge now. "We're starting to build a drying room tomorrow."

"A drying room?"

"Yeah. A place we hang herbs and shit to dry out so we can store it. We already have a small one, but we need something bigger. With the rate the mountain is calling people to her, we reckon our population will max out in the next couple of years."

"That's really interesting, and it sounds perfect for my piece. The main crux of my article is to highlight how you're all combating climate change with changes to your lifestyle in the homestead and your use of renewable resources as well as upcycling and reusing others to reduce your environmental footprint."

"Whoa, that's a whole lot of big words for this early in the morning. How about we just show you what we do and we'll leave the big fancy words to you?" Mason replies with a smirk. That earns a chuckle from all of us—even Nash.

I tilt my head to the side, shooting the twins a wink. "I think I can do that. You know, since it's my job and all."

"Great. So that's all sorted," Patti says. "If you need to speak with Gandalf or anybody else, just approach them and ask. They'll be more than happy to talk to you. We don't have any secrets here." She flashes me a smile. "Now, let's get you fed, and then you can wander around and *start* this story of yours."

"Thank you, Patty. I really appreciate it."

She smiles. "One thing to learn about the place, Faith. We're all family—blood and soul. We look out for each other and help out where we can. It's give and take. You've made Walker happier than I've ever seen him before. You've given us a proud and contented man who seems to have finally found the confidence he needed in running this homestead. It's wonderful to see. The least we can do is feed you and help you with your story. I know you'll pay us back in your own way eventually, especially since this place will be your home too one day."

I make a mental note to use that in the article—not the bit about making Walker happy, but the part about them all being family.

After eating Patty's delicious omelet, I'm ready to start my planning and research. And by the time Walker returns from the markets in the early afternoon, I have a plan of attack and a list a mile long of people to interview, and things to observe and/or do. This means I have a few hours spare to conduct some personal research of a different kind—mapping every single inch of Walker's body with my hands, mouth, and tongue. It's a glorious way to spend a Sunday evening before heading into a full-on work week.

Monday rolls around, I'm up early with Walker. And when we finally make it out of our cabin, I end up spending the morning with the twins, first watching, then helping build a new drying shed behind the Den. While they gathered materials and constructed the frame, I found out about their lives before coming to live at the homestead with their brothers and the rest of the founding sons.

"See, we were all born here," Mason says as he holds the frame steady and Miller hammers it in place. "But we left for whatever reason. Most of us went because our parents were a little..." Miller pauses his hammering and whistles like he's making the cuckoo sound, and Mason nods. "They kind of fell into a crazy, end of the world belief system in the final few years of their lives. So it drove a lot of us away, along with the other original homesteaders. Nash stayed. But the rest of us left, went to college, traveled a little. Then our folks passed, and we came back, which is when we all started working on making the homestead into what it was always meant to be—a society that lives in harmony with nature."

"You don't realize it when you're living the hectic city life," Miller adds. "But when you make your life about the land, you get this crazy sense of fulfillment that you can't get from anything you can buy from a shop.

Money, technology, popularity... it's all just stuff that can go away. But the land, nature—that's where you really find yourself."

"Sounds like the residents find a real sense of fulfillment living here," I muse as I take rushed notes about what they're saying.

"I think that's a fair summation," Mason says. Which is when I know I have my angle for the story.

A quick email sent to buttmunch outlining my intentions received a surprisingly supportive and positive response. So I decided to run with it, buoyed by my journalist brain working overtime at all the different things I could include in the feature, and even ideas for a series of human interest pieces about the men of the mountains and how they're giving back to the environment and future generations. Maybe I could even speak to Aster about doing a 'men behind the books' series?

Later that night, after dinner and a full body massage from Walker, which culminates in a *very* happy ending for both of us, I ask him about his childhood and growing up as the youngest of four boys to doomsday prepper parents.

"Doomsday preppers." He stretches back against his pillow and smiles. "That sounds very Mad Max. But yeah, that's what they became. In the beginning, it wasn't like that at all. There were four families—

Brady's, mine, and the twin's; then Jake and Nash's; Huxley and his mom; then finally there were Micah and Tate's family too. There were sixteen people living here to start with. Where The Den stands now was the only building, and we lived like one massive family. All of us kids lived wild and were free to roam and explore. But when we were teenagers, the adults decided to build a perimeter fence around the property and had everyone on guard duty." He shakes his head and pulls me in closer. "To this day, I don't know what sparked that. But bit by bit, the madness crept in until we weren't even allowed out of the compound—which is what they called it by then. For boys who wanted to grow up and get into trouble—you know, meet girls and all that—it was like a prison. So the moment we could get out, we did, and it wasn't until a few years ago that we came back."

"But Nash stayed?" I ask, leaning up on my elbow as I examine his expression while he speaks.

"He did. But not in the compound. He went down to Kenshaw and got a place of his own there. I guess part of why he became a cop was, so he had some sort of power to help fix things up here if it went bad. He was the one who found them too. They weren't his parents by blood, but they were all of our parents by community. I'm not sure he's ever gotten past it."

"What happened?"

"Fire. Linseed rags. They combusted while they were sleeping, set the whole place alight. Nash said they were still curled up together like they never knew it was coming."

"That's horrible. But oddly sweet too. Like, at least they went together," I say softly, and he nods.

"That's the comfort. I mean, sure, they went mad with their conspiracy theories. But they were still our parents, and we loved them. I wouldn't wish death on anyone. But if you've gotta go, at least let it be painless, right?"

"Do you ever worry you or your brothers will go mad?" I ask, more for myself than the story.

"No," he says with certainty in his voice. "None of us would let it happen. We're not living here to prepare for whatever apocalypse is coming, we're doing this to look after the land and protect our mountain for future generations."

By the time we finished our conversation and fell asleep in each other's arms, I had a really interesting perspective and deeper insight into the differences between an end of the world survivalist lifestyle, and the one all the residents promote here at Bear Mountain Homestead partake in. It's preparation and contingency-planning versus holistic living off the land, conservation, and preservation of the environment by leaving the least amount of impact on the mountain and the surrounding land. Like a lot of indigenous tribes, the principal belief of the community is to only use what is necessary while also protecting the flora and fauna around them. If anything, it makes me want to make this place my home more than ever. Of course, when I verbalized this to Walker in the morning, he rolls over and shows me just how much he liked my words in several delicious and satisfying ways.

Tuesday is my day with Nash. He takes me exploring Kenshaw's town limits and all the cute little businesses and features you'd expect in a small town of only one thousand people. Nash is one of three cops working out of Kenshaw, but Boone is the County Sheriff out of Woodward valley—the town at the base of Moose Mountain—and they're always available for backup in the ten-yearly event Kenshaw needs help. Walker met us for lunch at the Page in Time book, clothing, knick-knack, and baked goods store—it's a bit of a mishmash, but their food is amazing—which is where Nash left us, and Walker and I continued the tour on our own. Walker made a point of swinging by the school, the swimming pool which also doubles as an ice rink in the winter, the church, two restaurants that open on alternate days to share patrons equally, and finally, the Kenshaw Gazette, a small but surprisingly mighty district newspaper who have recently moved to a primarily online presence, with lots of established syndication deals with bigger publications around Alaska, Canada, and the lower 48. The Editor—a hippy-looking man called River Washington—seems interested in gaining another writer on his staff of one. So I left with some extra hope and Walker left with a spring in his step.

"See? The mountain wants you here," he says as I slide the card with River's email address into my pocket. "It's all coming together."

"Seems that way. I just have to hope he likes the writing samples I send through."

"Oh, he will. How could he not? You're the amazing Faith Marie Johnson—soon to be Long—he'll be lucky to have you and he knows it."

"Soon to be Long, huh?"

He flashes me a grin. "Gotta make an honest woman out of you, sweetheart. The rate we're going, there'll be a baby swelling that belly of yours in no time."

"Were you planning on asking me?" I have to fight my own smile as I glance at him adoringly.

"Of course." He lifts my hand to his lips and kisses my knuckles. "And I will. When the time is right."

"Now I'm going to be expecting it constantly," I say with a laugh.

"That'll be part of the fun—knowing but not knowing. Maybe while we're here we should shop rings?"

I bite my lip as a blush heats my cheeks. "OK."

When Wednesday rolls around, Serena and Brady return from their honeymoon. The moment Serena saw me, she squealed like a stuck pig and hugged me so tight I could barely breathe. So now she's all aboard the 'get Faith to stay at the homestead' train, going above and beyond to show me everything and anything I could ever need to know about life on the homestead and the mountain. She even commandeered Marta and her toddler daughter, Vera, to drive me to Woodward Valley, where I met Aster Hollingsworth in the flesh.

"I am such a huge fan of yours," I gush, feeling almost like I'm meeting the queen as I shake her hand.

"And I'm a fan of yours," she says with a knowing smile. "Word is, my next book involves a reporter who moves to the mountain after falling in love with the most loyal of the Long brothers."

My heart beats wildly with excitement. "How does it end?" I ask, desperately wanting some guidance as I realize that Aster must be to Moose Mountain what Gandalf is to Bear Mountain. *I can't believe I didn't connect those dots before now.*

"That's something you'll have to experience for yourself," she says kindly. "But I can tell you it'll all work out for you and Walker. And I can also promise you an early copy of the book. Signed, of course."

"Oh my. Thank you so much, Aster. That means...a lot. Thank you." I feel dumb the way I gush, but it's not every day you meet one of your idols.

On top of meeting Aster, I also get the chance to meet the other women whose stories were foretold in Aster's mountain man series. All of them are now married to and creating families with the Cooper men—the original protectors of Moose Mountain, where the magic and prophecies truly began.

By Thursday, I'm hunched over my computer typing up a storm. I have all of my notes and research, and my story is half done. And with buttmunch subbing my progress daily, and Giles even checking in with me, the pressure is truly on.

"Want me to get your meals sent up here for you today?" Walker asks as he places a steaming mug of coffee in front of me and presses a gentle kiss against the side of my head. *Have I mentioned he's the best?*

"No. I still need to get out there and talk to Gandalf before I can wrap this up. So I'll grab something then. Thank you, though. You're the treasure of the mountain, Walker Long."

"Speaking of treasure," he says, reaching into his pocket for something. FOr a moment, my breath catches and I cease all work, wondering if this will be the moment he proposes after teasing me with it for days. But instead, he places an old arrowhead on the table next to me. My heart almost deflated, but then he told me the story to go with it. "When the boys and I were young, we went through a phase of making our own bows and arrows to hunt with. Mason and Miller found one when they were building the new drying shed."

"That's so cool," I say, turning it over in my fingers. "Thank you."

He leans down and presses his mouth to mine. "Thank you," he murmurs when we part. There's a temptation to forget the article and go right back to bed, but somehow we both resist. "I'll leave you so we can both get some work done."

"If you must," I sigh.

"I must," he says with a wink as he pulls his coat and boots on. "Have fun talking to Tim. He's eccentric, but he's also a riot."

Turning back to my coffee, I check the time as I sip at my coffee. If I can get the draft mostly done by lunchtime, I can meet with Gandalf which will give me twenty-four hours to finish the article and send it through to Marvin. I love being ahead of my deadline.

"ARE you sure you're not taking me the long way to the mountaintop?" I pant, bending at the waist and resting my hands on my knees, trying to catch my breath after taking what I can only assume is the scenic route to the top of Bear Mountain. Gandalf looks back at me over his shoulder, not looking even remotely tired despite being at least forty years older than me. *This mountain air must be like the fountain of youth for your lungs.*

"C'mon, Faith. You're supposed to be young and sprightly, not outdone by an old man with a cane."

I narrow my eyes at him. "You don't have a ca—" My mouth gapes open when he whips out a wooden stake from his side, my brain struggling to compute where the hell he pulled that from.

"You had that hidden somewhere, didn't you?"

He smirks and winks at me. "I guess that's for me to know and you to wonder about. Anyway, we're here, it's just over the crest." He points ahead on the trail.

True to his word, three minutes and one stitch in my side later, we finally reach the top of the mountain and sit on a beautifully carved hardwood bench set into the dirt.

"So, you want to talk about the mountain, the prophecy, and the spirit that surrounds all the protectors of the land in these parts?"

I chuckle, not surprised that the Seer already knows what this interview is about before I even open my mouth.

"*Or,* would you like to know whether you get to stay on the mountain and not have to leave the side of your beloved soulmate?" Now my eyes are wide and bugging out at the man. If ever I doubted his ability to see into the future, I don't now.

"Um..."

"Or, is it a bit of column A and a bit of column B?"

I hold up my hand. "OK, now you're just freaking me out."

"That is not my intention. I only seek to bring the founding sons and their true loves together."

"So, you can tell me what's going to happen between Walker and me?"

"Yes. But with some limitations. I can only offer you guidance. The choices you make must be yours."

"What kind of guidance?"

"About your career; about this story you're writing with the best of intentions. Or we can discuss whether you should give up your life in the city for a man you've just met. Whether you'll find true happiness on the mountain..." he rumbles, his raspy voice somehow soothing even when his words are freaking me out. *Get out of my head, Gandalf.*

"That's a lot of things I could ask about. Is there also a limit to how many answers I get?" He simply smiles at that, so I'm going to take it as a yes which means my choices here are pretty limited. If I want to get this article finished with time to spare, I need to focus on why we came up here."Um... I guess what I really need to know is whether you believe that the prophecy activated by Martie and Van having Vera, really will extend to all the founding sons, and why—"

"Why the soulmates feel pain when they are apart?" Gandalf stares into my eyes as I talk, his eyes widening with realization. "That's easy, my sweet girl. It's because they belong together. I suppose you could look at it as an insurance policy for the mountain. The founding brothers are tied spiritually to the mountain, and their soulmates are bonded spiritually to them. It keeps you together and makes you more willing to fight those obstacles that undoubtedly crop up in your journey to each other."

"An insurance policy? Do you mean it's the mountain's way of keeping us all here?"

"It is. The mountain is where your heart and your happiness lies. Together, you can leave the mountain, but you'll always feel restless without it. You can ask my sister Patty about that. She and her husband, Rick, left Moose Mountain when their children were young, and while they loved seeing and experiencing the wide world, it's the mountain that eventually won them all back. It's where we belong, and the mountain only calls those who belong."

"Would you describe the mountain as a utopia?"

"For those who belong, most definitely."

"Um...you mentioned before that there would be obstacles before I finally settle on the mountain. What kind of things could I expect, and how would one prepare herself for them?."

Gandalf reaches out and covers my hands with his. "Now *that* my child would be telling you too much. All I can do as the Seer of the mountain is listen to the mountain's spirit and impart the wisdom she shares with me. For you and Walker, I cannot yet see where the path to happiness will lead because it is still murky, which means..."

"Obstacles are coming our way."

He nods, letting that news sink in. "One obstacle, one that will take—excuse the pun—*faith* to overcome."

"Does that mean it will take faith as in trust, or faith as in *me*?"

Gandalf closes his eyes and hums faintly, but does not reply directly. "All I will say, Faith, is that it will take great strength in character to overcome whatever difficulty is coming, a strong will and fortitude too. But I believe in you and Walker, you are a true love pairing, you both bring out the best in each other. You make him believe in himself and he..."

"What? He what?"

"That is something that you will realize when you beat whatever it is that stands in your way."

And that, as far as our conversation goes, is that. Gandalf stands and steers his body back toward the homestead. And I have little choice but to follow because I don't want to get lost and because I have a lot more thinking to do while I finish up with this story.

Just as I suspected, the trip home down the mountain only took ten minutes, which means he totally took me the longest, most tiring way possible to get to the top. Even despite that, I'm feeling happier than I ever have in my entire life and it has everything to do with Walker, the homestead, and the smiling face of my best friend who's waiting for me outside the Den with a glass of the mountain's first wine vintage when Gandalf and I finally get back. The old man's words from our talk definitely gave me food for thought for the rest of the day, though.

Lucky for me, Walker proved to be a great distraction, and an even better provider of food, drink, and moral support when later that night, I set up my laptop at the small dining table in the cabin and set out to write the final draft of my story about Bear Mountain Homestead: Saving the environment for future generations one resource at a time.

16

WALKER

"Where are you taking me?" Faith asks, meeting me outside the cabin dressed in her snow gear just as I asked. It's her last night on the mountain before she goes back to Anchorage to convince buttmunch—I literally have no idea what this guy's name is—to let her work remotely so she can move here permanently.

She emailed the final draft off to him less than an hour ago and hasn't stopped smiling since. She seems super proud of her work and I'm proud of her too, especially after seeing how hard she works and the effort she expends to get her story. I'm in awe and feeling fucking lucky that I get to call this wonderful woman mine. If this buttmunch guy can't see what a talent he has on his payroll, then the Kenshaw Gazette will be more than happy to have a gifted reporter like Faith on their team, because no matter what comes next in her career, it'll involve moving to the mountain. Of that, I've no doubt.

"I'm taking you somewhere cold," I say, grinning as I secure the pack with food and supplies on the back of the snowmobile.

She gestures to her warmly dressed body as she grins at me with bright pink cheeks. "I gathered that...unless you just like me well-covered."

"Hop on," I say, chuckling and nodding to the vehicle before I climb on front. She slides her leg over the rear of the seat and wraps her arms around my waist before I start the electric engine and steer us off the homestead, jetting us a little higher up the mountain to a smaller secluded cabin we built years ago at a natural lookout with a perfect view of the Northern Lights. With Thanksgiving fast approaching, it's the perfect time of the year to see them in all their magnificence. And also the perfect place for a mountain proposal. I have the ring I bought in Kenshaw tucked in my pocket, so tonight is the night I make this official. I'm not letting her leave this mountain without knowing how sure I am about this relationship.

There's a few squeals of laughter as we speed along the trail, a close call with a low-hanging branch giving us both an adrenaline boost before we arrive at our destination shortly after.

The moment I stop the snowmobile, Faith gets off and spreads her arms wide. "Wow. It's a mini-cabin with a view!"

Moving in behind her, I circle her waist and press my frozen lips to her warm neck, causing her to giggle and squirm. "When the sun sets, we'll see the lights up here too."

"Really?" she gasps and turns to meet my eyes. "You know, I've seen them so many times in my life, but they never cease to amaze me. I'm so glad you have a special place to see it from the mountain."

"The mountain always provides, sweetheart. Anything you need, even an awesome view."

She turns in my arms and loops her hands around the back of my neck, staring deep into my eyes. "You're the only view I need," she whispers, pressing her lips to mine and kissing me with so much passion that it warms the both of us up.

"Let's get this stuff inside so I can build us a fire and feed you before I fuck you."

"Fuck me, feed me, and keep me forever," she whispers, rubbing her nose against mine.

"In that order?"

She smiles up at me. "Yeah. I think I want it in that order."

"Your wish is my command, sweetheart," I say, lacing my fingers with hers as I hoist our pack off the snow-mobile and we both head into the cabin. It's a tiny icebox right now, but once I have a fire roaring in the hearth, the place warms up nice and fast.

"OK. So what do we have in here?" Faith asks as she unpacks the containers of food, blankets, and... "Champagne?" Her eyes meet mine and she grins. "What could this possibly be for?"

"I thought we'd celebrate the submission of your story in style. And..." I reach into my pocket and approach her. "I was going to wait until after we'd eaten, but since you changed the order of things..." I lower myself to one knee then hold the velvet box up to her, opening the lid to reveal a flower-shaped diamond ring inside.

"Oh my gosh," she gasps, covering her mouth with her hands. "I knew this was coming, but seeing you on one knee...Oh my god, Walker. I love you so much, baby."

"I love you too, sweetheart," I say, taking her shaking hand in mine after I pull the ring from the box and hold it between two fingers. "Faith Marie Johnson, from the moment I saw you, I knew you were destined to be mine. I fell, and I fell hard. And now I can't imagine living any part of my life without you. I know you have to go back down the mountain for a while tomorrow. But I want you to know that I'm right here waiting for you, ready to make you my wife the moment you return. Will you marry me, Faith?"

"Yes, Walker, yes!" she cries, launching herself at me the moment I slide the ring on her finger.

Our lips collide, our tongues seeking each other out as our hands make fast work removing our clothes while we move toward the bed, touching and teasing each other with renewed urgency, our heightened emotions making this moment feel more important than any other time we've been together before.

"I have something I want to tell you," Faith gasps as my mouth moves down her body, licking and tasting. "Something important."

"You can tell me anything." I run my tongue in a circle around her belly button before I push her knees up, inhaling the sweet scent of her arousal.

"I'm not leaving."

"What?" I lift my head, meeting her eyes as she smiles and runs a gentle hand over my cheek and into my hair.

"I said I'm not going home. Not yet, anyway. Marvin loved the article and said I can write a whole series about the mountain."

"Marvin? Is that buttmunch?"

She laughs as she nods. "That's him. I thought you and me could go into Anchorage together at Thanksgiving, take a few days packing up my apartment, and spend the holiday at my parents' house in Kinleyville on the way back. I'd like for you to meet them before the wedding." A renewed giggle bounces her beautiful tits. "We're getting married. My mom is going to lose her mind."

"Yes," I say quickly.

"Yes, my mom will lose her mind?"

"No, well yes, probably." I laugh. "But yes, I'll come to Anchorage with you for Thanksgiving. With Brady back, they can spare me a few days, and I'd like to officially ask your father for your hand."

Faith's eyes go soft at that, glistening wet as she smiles up at me and slides her fingers deeper into my hair. "What will you do if he says no?"

"Steal you away to the mountain, anyway. There is no other option."

"I love you so much, Walker," she whispers.

"I love you too, Faith," I return, just before I lower my head and sweep my tongue through her seam, showing how deeply I feel for her with my mouth, my hands, and my body until we're exhausted and starved. Then I feed her and do it all again because this time I get to keep her. *Fuck me, feed me, then keep me forever.* The words she said earlier in the night reverberate in my ears.

Oh, I intend to, sweetheart. Forever and then some.

17

FAITH

I wake the next morning with a full heart, an aching body, and a smile on my face. Last night with Walker was *glorious*. In fact, I think I'll propose we spend another day or two here. Another day or two of uninterrupted alone time with my new fiance could be just what the doctor ordered, and I'm sure Brady won't mind filling in since Walker steps up for Brady without complaint whenever it's needed. I think Walker deserves this time off after doing the work of two men since Brady and Serena got married.

Now that I've told Walker I'm staying, I feel closer to both him and the mountain than ever before. I just can't wipe the smile off my face. But why should I? As I hold up my hand and admire the gorgeous jewelry on my ring finger, I know this is just the start of a life filled with happiness and joy.

Turning my head, I find Walker splayed out beside me, lying on his stomach, his toned arms bent under his pillow, his face so peaceful. But even asleep, his lips are tipped up, and god do I love that I'm the reason he's so happy.

Not wanting to disturb him—because lord knows he needs as much rest as possible after the impressive amount of effort he expended both in *and* out of the bedroom last night. His sexual prowess has earned him a little more shut-eye—I carefully slide off the mattress and pull on a clean pair of underwear from my bag then grab Walker's flannel shirt from the floor and slip it over my head before tip-toeing out into the other room where my phone is charging.

Picking it up, I lean against the small kitchen counter with a huge window pointed toward the lookout, smiling to myself because we never did take the time to look at the Northern Lights. We got so caught up in each other, our eyes never left this cabin. *Maybe we can make up for that tonight.* I'm still smiling as I press the power button to turn my cell on. As soon as it boots up and I enter my pin code, I'm hit with notification after notification in rapid succession. I quickly switch it to silent mode, my brows knitted together as I see four missed calls from Giles, as well as two text messages from him asking for me to call back immediately. Assuming there was something wrong with my story—like maybe the email didn't go through on Friday for some reason—I open my email app to check for a delivery report. Sure enough, it's right there, the newspaper's server acknowledging receipt of my story on Friday three minutes after I sent it.

Spotting my padded ski pants and boots hanging up by the cabin's front door, I quickly put them all on and phone in hand, quietly slip outside and move toward the trail, just far enough to not disturb Walker's sleep while I call the office.

The phone rings five times before going to Giles's voicemail, advising that he is out of contact until Tuesday and to direct all newspaper related calls to buttmunch. With my investigative brain needing to get to the bottom of this mystery, I decide to try the paper's number, hoping to catch one of the on-call weekend reporters at their desks so I can double-check that there's no issue with my article.

"Anchorage Press news desk. This is Grant."

I huff out a huge sigh of relief. "Hey Grant, it's Faith."

"Faith! How are you? I must say the office is way duller without your bright spark lighting up the newsroom."

"Aww, I miss you all too. But you know, this mountain is—"

"Beautiful, distracting, *thrilling*?"

I giggle and shake my head, the weight on my finger reminding me of just how amazing the mountain, the people, and especially a certain sleeping man inside, truly are. "Yeah, you have *no* idea."

"I bet. You can tell me all about it when you're back in the office. That's tomorrow, right?"

"Ah, I'm staying put for a while. Marvin gave me the go-ahead to do a series on the Homestead. Hey, do you know when my homestead article is running? Will it be included in Wednesday's edition, or is he saving it for next Sunday's fluff piece?"

"I don't know, but I can check for you. Give me just a minute." He goes quiet and I can hear the tapping of keys on the other end. "Ahhh, wow. It looks like they put a rush on it and it's the lead story on this morning's online edition, but it didn't make it in time for the print edition, so that's going in tomorrow. Way to go, Faith!" I freeze in place, my hand almost dropping the phone at my ear.

"Wait...what?" I put my hand over my mouth, my smile stretching from ear to ear. I never imagined my story was inspiring enough to make the *lead.*

"You heard it right, my friend. It's right here: *Mountain Homesteaders: Climate Change Pioneers, Doomsday Whack Jobs, or a Dangerous Cult?* Whoa, that's one powerful headline. Hope you're staying safe up there. These guys sound *nuts.*"

"What did you say that headline was?" Surely that wasn't right.

"*Mountain Homesteaders: Climate Change Pioneers, or Doomsday Whack Jobs, or a Dangerous Cult?*" he repeats, letting me know I *didn't* hear him wrong. *Crap.*

If brains could explode, mine would've just detonated all over the mountain top. "Grant, that's not right! That's not my story!"

"It says right here, *a special investigation by Faith M Johnson*. So unless there's been a big miscommunication somewhere along the line, that's exactly the story that's going to press tomorrow."

"No, no no no no no," I chant, pacing back and forth in the snow, one hand gripping the phone tight, the other raking through my hair, nearly pulling the strands clean out. "I need that story taken down. Right now."

"You know I can't do that, Faith. I don't have that kind of power."

"Then put me through to Buttm—I mean, I need Marvin."

"He's out of the office for the weekend. You know he doesn't work weekends."

"Then give me his home phone number, Grant. Please, it's urgent."

"I don't have it. I mean, *no one* has that. You know he's a stickler for having time outside of the office and not being disturbed. Yes, I like you more than him, but I also like my job, and I like getting *paid*. So, even if I could, I can't help you."

"Shit. OK. Yeah, I get that Grant. It's just that is *not* the headline I suggested. Hell, it's not even the *premise* of my damn story. These people aren't whack jobs or even survivalists. That story *can't* keep circulating, and it definitely can't go to *press*. It's not only wrong, it's—" Oh my god, this will devastate everyone on the homestead. They'll think I'm no better than some tabloid hack who used them to write a story to further my career. And Serena, oh no. No way can I do this to her, or Brady, or especially Walker. *How am I going to fix this?*

Then it hits me. There's only one way my story could be this screwed up. I can't believe Giles would twist my words to make me look foolish, so the only person willing and able to do that to me is buttmunch himself, Marvin Markle. He was *far* too accommodating this whole trip: the story, my research, and suggestions—all of it. He easily accepted first my outline, and then my updates. Come to think about it, I don't remember seeing any subedits in my inbox either. What if he never planned to publish my story all along? What if he has been sabotaging me this whole time, and this is the final pièce de résistance in his plan to get me back for being the paid intern dumped in his lap? Which means I have little to no hope of stopping the story —*his* version—of hitting newsstands first thing tomorrow morning. An online version can be taken down, but once those printed papers get out there, there's no taking it back. If that happens, the life I envisaged for myself here on the mountain, living the rest of my days by Walker's side and with Serena as my best friend *and* my sister-in-law, would be impossible, because not only would the homesteaders not want me here, the mountain spirit who has been so giving to me, would probably curse me if I even stepped foot back on her land.

Which means I have one shot to make this right. I need to get into that office and stop this myself.

"Faith? Are you still there?"

"Yeah. I am. But, Grant, I'm going to need your help. You know how the Christmas party this year is happening at Giles's estate? I need you to text me a copy of the invite."

"You're not showing up there on a weekend, are you?"

"I have to, Grant. I can't have my name attached to something that could hurt these people or the man I love. I need you to help me stop this."

"The man you love? Well, if it's love on the line, I'm all in. The invite should hit your cell at any moment."

I feel the vibration beneath my palm. "Thank you, Grant. I owe you one."

"Just invite me to your wedding and we'll call it even."

"Deal," I say, taking a deep fortifying breath as I jump on the snowmobile and make my way back to the homestead, hoping to God I can fix this before anyone I care about finds out. There is zero time to waste.

18

WALKER

The cold creeps in, signaling the dwindling fire. I'm about to get up and throw more wood on when I realize I'm colder than I should be. *Where's the warm body that should be pressed against me?*

Suddenly, I'm wide awake and staring at the empty bed beside me. *Where the hell did Faith go?* I call out her name, hoping that maybe she's just visiting the bathroom. But I know that's just wishful thinking since there isn't even an ounce of warmth on the sheets beside me. *What the actual fuck?*

I get out of bed and look for the flannel shirt Faith nearly ripped off me last night, but it's nowhere to be found. Instead, I grab my pants, pulling them on before grabbing a sweater and tugging that over my head as well. "Faith?" I keep calling her name and getting no response. But it doesn't stop me from trying.

The cabin is tiny and there are only two places she could be—in here or out there. And she's definitely not in here.

Pulling back the curtain, the first thing that hits me are the tracks leading away from where the snowmobile used to be. The electric motor is a hell of a lot better for the environment than one that requires gas, but the fucker is quiet as a mouse. Now Faith is gone, and I didn't even hear her leave, and she certainly didn't take the time to say goodbye. But I think the biggest question here is, why did she leave in the first place? And the second biggest is, when, or *is*, she coming back?

I'm trying to keep my cool here. I'm trying to convince myself that she just went back to the Homestead for some more supplies. But the thundering ache in my chest is telling me otherwise. I place my hands on my hips and pace the floor, taking deep breaths to calm down. *In through the nose, out through the mouth.* I do this several times and it doesn't do a lot to quell the panic that keeps clawing up my neck.

"*Fuck*," I thunder, picking up a chair and throwing it across the room in a fit of frustrated rage. It hits against the wall and clatters to the ground in pieces, but it doesn't make me feel better. Not by a long shot. Faith has left the mountain, I can feel the loss deep in my heart. I rub my chest, trying to quell the ache but it won't stop, I know the only way to end this pain is to be close to my One. She promised me she was staying and now she's gone. *What the fucking fuck?*

With my blood boiling beneath my skin, I get my shit together and ready myself to trek back to the Home-stead through the thick layer of snow that fell overnight. It'll take me at least three times as long to get back down there on foot than it would on the snowmobile. *Why did she take it? Why did she leave? Did I do something wrong? Was the proposal too soon? I thought we were on the same page...*

A hundred scenarios have run through my head by the time I finally make it back to the homestead. I've gone from convincing myself this is all a joke and she's hiding in the cabin to surprise me, to thinking she used me to get a story and never had any intention of staying here like she said. I've gone from the dark to the light and everywhere in between, and by the time walking past the first cabin, I'm more confused than when I first discovered her gone. But mostly, I'm pissed and I'm freezing, and I'm trying to restrain myself from losing my shit completely until I get some actionable information. With my cell still in my cabin, all I can think is to get to it so I can call her and demand some kind of explanation—or at least find out what the hell is going on. Last I checked, it's not normal practice to take off on your fiance the morning after you get engaged unless there's a damn good reason.

Just as I turn toward my cabin, Mason and Miller come running towards me, yelling like a couple of panicked school kids. "Where the hell did she go?" they demand in unison.

"That's something I'd like to know myself," I say, continuing on my way, my teeth clenched tight.

Mason stops me with a firm grip on my arm. "Did you know, brother?" His eyes are narrowed slits, and it hits me that it's not panic I'm seeing, it's swirling anger. *What the hell?*

"Know what? That she was planning on abandoning me on the lookout? No. I fucking didn't. Now, if you don't mind, I have some shit to take care of."

"We're talking about the article, Walk," Miller says, handing me a tablet and tapping the screen to wake it up. "She made out that we're a bunch of psychotic Doomsday Preppers who believe in magic. It says we're a cult. Brady is ropeable."

Staring at the screen in disbelief, I scan the article, my stomach bottoming out with each scathing remark I read. My eyes burn and my skin heats. "This can't be right," I grate out. "She wouldn't do this."

"Well, it's her name on the byline, brother," Mason argues. "You can't pretend that tidbit isn't staring you in the face."

"Is this *really* how she sees us, Walk?" Miller asks, the calmer of the two, and I hate that I don't have an answer for that. I thought she loved the Homestead. I thought she wanted to live here with us—with *me*. I thought she wanted to make a life together here on the mountain. Was it all a lie? A ruse? Some kind of joke to play on a naïve man, desperate enough to believe a spirit would send his soulmate to him? Maybe Nash is the only one of us with any sense here. *Shit. I can't breathe.*

"I need to go," I mutter, my head reeling and my chest tightening like a vice, threatening to squeeze the life out of me. I thrust the tablet back in Miller's hands and stalk toward my cabin. I just need to get to my damn phone and I can finally find out what the hell is happening.

"Brady wants to see you ASAP."

I release a sardonic laugh and shake my head while I continue walking. "Tell Brady he can fuck right off. I've got my own shit to deal with, I don't need it from him too."

"Walker," Mason calls after me before Miller tells him to let me go.

"You know how hard Brady is on him. He's right, he doesn't need that right now."

And that's the last I hear before I close myself behind my cabin door and grab my cell, dialing Faith's number before I can even take a breath. The question on constant repeat in my head is, *why?* Why did she do this? I can't connect the beautiful, radiant, joyful Faith I had in my arms just a few hours ago, to the reporter who would write absolute garbage about the homestead, my family, and our beloved mountain.

I thought we were supposed to be forever, and now...now I'm wondering if I'm ever going to see her again...

19

FAITH

On the floor of my apartment with my back leaning against the sofa, I stare ahead at nothing. The TV blares in the background, but I can barely make out the sounds. I don't see its flickering colors. I don't see or hear *anything.* I can only stare ahead in a daze, my head full of mistakes and misguided trust, of broken promises, of letting down people I've come to care about—including the love of my life. The weight of my engagement ring on my finger is heavy and tight, mimicking the claustrophobic ache in my chest where my heart beats in constricted silence.

There's no thumping against my ribs, there's no warmth where there has been ever since I first laid eyes on Walker Long. There's just a cold gnawing throb deep inside me that I've felt ever since I drove off the mountain. I was warned of the pain felt when two soulmates are apart once they'd been together, but I never imagined such debilitating, mind-numbing discomfort that makes it impossible to ignore.

Not that I want to forget about Walker, or the homestead, or the mountain. I desperately wish I was back in our cabin, snuggled under the covers, my fiance lying beside me, cloaking me with his warmth, and making me feel so loved, so safe, so happy. A stark contrast to how I am now. I can't remember the last time I moved, let alone ate. Drinking, though, now *that* I have done.

Tears sting my eyes as I remember just how fruitless my attempt was to stop Marvin's hacked version of my homestead story from going to press. The bastard didn't even have the balls to turn up at the office yesterday morning, having put in an emergency leave of absence at the last minute. So now it's Tuesday, my phone is *still* ringing off the hook, my inbox is full, and I'm still here, sitting on the floor, drinking my bottle of wine, contemplating a change of scenery, country, career, *life*...anything to escape the giant mess of a disaster I find myself in. *They must hate me.*

Tears sting my eyes when I think of Walker. He must be feeling so betrayed, so humiliated, so angry, and hurt. And there's the pain...*oh my god*, if he's feeling even half as bad as I do, he must be positively miserable. I want to go to him. But I can't. I can't even bring myself to talk to him. Not yet. I haven't answered a single phone call or replied to any of his messages with anything other than a simple, *sorry* via text. That's it. Just one word. Because what else is there to say? The story went live on the website while Walker proposed to me, then it went to press the very next morning and for all my driving around, yelling and screaming and threatening...there was *nothing* I could do about it. And to make matters worse, the damn thing has gone viral according to my social media notifications. *Great.*

Needless to say, I feel horrible. I feel empty and hollow inside. I feel....like a failure. And it's all because a man with a chip on his shoulder and an apparent distaste for me and my work, decided to twist the narrative of a feel-good human interest piece into a scandalous—and completely false—exposé to further his agenda. He didn't even stick around to face the music—or me.

Meeting with Giles yesterday, he seemed very uneasy over the situation and was trying to track down buttmunch to demand an explanation. Thankfully, I was able to show Giles my original outline and the final version of the story that was submitted for publication. To say he was understanding and supportive is an understatement. Having the Owner and Chief Editor of your publication go to bat for you is definitely a nod of confidence, and it feels good to know he's doing everything he can to claw back the story. But once something gets syndicated and goes viral, all bets are off. There's not much that can be done to correct that narrative and cancel out all the lies. To make matters worse, Marvin is out of the office until *after* Thanksgiving, citing a family emergency he has to attend to. We're all doubtful, but nothing can be done about the sabotage of my work and the damage to my career until he returns to the office to face the music. *Buttmunch!*

It's like a media snowball that's slowly but surely gaining momentum as it rolls down the hill, picking up speed and collecting anybody and everybody in its way as it goes. Including Aster, who had to issue a press statement negating everything stated in the article. Marvin had twisted my words to insinuate that an internationally bestselling author had been brain-washing women with her work about delusional mountain men. He claimed she had dangerously encouraged and boosted the ungodly cause of the homestead, or as he called it "the Bear Mountain Survivalist Camp."

I lift the wine bottle to my lips again and close my eyes, wishing I could be like Dorothy and snap my heels together to disappear to another world, just until I can come up with a way to make this right for everyone—especially for my handsome mountain man fiance.

He said I make him want to be better, to *do* better. What I never said was that he makes me feel like I *am* better, that I'm more than I am, like a cherished princess who can do anything she sets her mind to. His support was unwavering, his love unwaning, and now...I hate to think how he sees me now.

I left him a note in our cabin before I fired Bertha up and snuck away off the homestead. Just something I wanted to say to at least give him some hope that I could—would—make everything right again. But now...even that note is a lie. Because I couldn't stop it. I couldn't stop the world from being told that Alaska is hiding the next 'People's Temple'. Memes about mountain man Kool-Aid are already circulating, people are laughing at them, *fearing* them, and it's all my fault. *How am I supposed to go back there now?*

Then a light bulb goes off, and for the first time in hours, I'm pushing myself up off my living room floor and reaching for my phone, since I left my laptop up the mountain when I left in such a rush.

It may not work—because let's be honest, people love a scandal more than the truth—but if I can make a video and tell the world straight from my heart about my own experience at the homestead, give them a truthful account with pictures to *show* them the time I spent there, the things I did, the people I met, the life I was—*am*—ready to start with Walker, then maybe I can give the world a different perspective. Giles is printing my original article along with a retraction in tomorrow's edition, so in the age of social media and meme sharing, maybe a heartfelt video will do something to right the wrongs that Marvin Markle inflicted on the kind, loving, welcoming people of the Bear Mountain Homestead.

It has to be worth a shot, right?

And if by some miracle this works, then maybe I can grovel my way back into Walker's life. Beg him to take me back, work on earning his trust again. Because one thing is absolutely clear, the mountain doesn't fuck around with this painful separation business. Walker and I *must* be destined to be together if the burning ache in my heart is anything to go by.

With the love of my life in mind, I'm more determined than ever to do whatever it takes to make it up to the people on the mountain. *My* people. My future home. I have to believe there is still good in this world. Our happiness depends on it.

20

WALKER

"I can't believe she'd do this," Serena says as she drops the newspaper on the table in front of her. "This is so unlike her. I've never known her to act with anything but honesty and integrity in her work."

I've finally come to her and Brady's cabin to face the music after hiding myself away from everyone for a day and getting blind drunk. Surprisingly, Brady isn't tearing me a new one. He's pissed, sure—there have been people picketing outside the entrance to the homestead all morning—but he's not directing that anger at me. Which is a nice change since the last time I messed up, I caused a greenhouse to collapse and he reamed me out for days.

"If she didn't do it," Brady says. "Then who did? There's a lot of information in here that had to come from her. It's twisted. But it's based on her experience." He frowns suddenly and looks over his shoulder out the window. "Oh, my god. Can we call Nash and ask him to do something about those protesters? I can barely hear myself think."

"They have a right to protest," I mutter, feeling half-dead inside without Faith being close to me. "And they're not on our land. So we can't do anything."

He gets up and leans on the windowsill, "This is fucking ridiculous. Has anyone gotten hold of Faith to get this retracted yet?" The picketers are out there chanting and holding signs saying things like, 'Save the Children' or 'don't drink the Kool-Aid', and 'the mountain isn't god' among other things. It's no one from the local towns, of course, just a bunch of woke people traveling around picking up whatever cause comes their way. They'll be picketing somewhere else soon enough, but it's seriously messing with morale in the meantime. Some of the residents are afraid to go outside in case things escalate. The entire reason they came here was for the peace and quiet the homestead provided. And now Nash is telling us there are rumblings at the station about a search warrant coming from above so they can come and check us out thoroughly. It's getting out of hand.

"I've tried calling Faith at home, at work, and even at her parents, but I can't get a hold of her," Serena says. "Walker hasn't had any luck either. I even asked Dad to call, but he tried and got her voicemail. She's gone silent for now."

“She sent me a text that said, sorry,” I say, flipping the newspaper face down. I don’t want to see that headline anymore.

Serena huffs out a relieved sigh. “Well, that’s something, I guess. But it’s no admission of guilt. The way I see it, the only person who had access to her notes and her story was her boss. And he's had it in for her since the start. So maybe this is his way of finally getting rid of her? We call him buttmunch for a reason.”

“I guess that’s a possibility,” Brady says. “But with Faith refusing contact, it’s a little difficult to find out what really went down. I think the best course of action here is to just trust in the mountain. And Walk, you’ve gotta trust your heart. The mountain sent her to you for a reason. She’s your One. So, I think you should go to Gandalf for some guidance. And failing that, you’ve gotta get down to Anchorage and find her. No matter what the reason behind these...these *lies*.” He gestures to the folded newspaper and scowls. “You still need her in your life. I don’t even know what happens when a mated pair are apart for too long. Van and Martie were apart for almost three months, and they said it felt like dying. Serena and I were apart for a few weeks and that felt impossible. I’d hate to imagine what would happen if Faith never came back. You’ve gotta go find her, brother. Forget the article, forget the asshole protestors. Focus on the woman you fell in love with. The homestead will support you.”

Blowing out my breath, I slowly nod. I'm as angry about this article as everyone else is. But I have to agree with Serena, this doesn't feel like something Faith would do. So after finishing my conversation with Brady, I head out of the cabin and seek out Gandalf. I find him behind The Den, pulping apples to make cold-pressed juice, which he claims is the secret to his widely enjoyed hooch.

"Think you can spare a moment to talk?" I ask, picking up one of the glass gallon jugs to hold under the spout of the press for him.

"If you keep helping me like that, I'll have all the time in the world for you," the old man says, smiling at me as he pants with the exertion of turning the crank.

"Want me to do the strenuous part and you can just hold this?" I ask, causing him to pause and chuckle.

"That would make a lot more sense. Youth before beauty, huh?" He winks and I give him the first smile I've managed to crack in the last few days as we switch positions. "What is it you wanted to speak to me about, Walker?" he asks once the apple juice is flowing from the spout.

"I wanted to talk to you about Faith. She left as soon as that article was published and none of us have heard from her since."

"I read that article. A lot of baseless untruths in there." He flashes me a smile. "What did you think about it?"

"I don't know. It made me mad, I guess. Mad and hurt. Cheated. I'd actually... I proposed to her the night before. We were going to go to Anchorage and pack up her apartment together, spend Thanksgiving meeting her parents. But now..." I shrug as I sweep the remnants of the pressed apple into the compost bag and reload the chute. "Brady thinks I should just go and talk to her face-to-face. She's not answering anyone's calls or messages, and we can't get hold of her through the newspaper. Some guy called Grant seems to be her gatekeeper there and won't put anyone through... so, I guess I need some of your sage advice and guidance. You're always the one with the answers around here. What should I do?"

He remains quiet as he spoons yeast inside the bottle, then affixes the airlock to cap it off, glancing up at me as he sets the finished bottle of hooch-to-be aside. "I think you should trust your heart. The mountain will guide you."

I drop my hands to my sides, my palms slapping against my thighs as I stare at Gandalf agape. "That's probably the *least* helpful thing you've ever said to me," I say as I step away and shake my head. "I came to you for some sort of help—a little wisdom—and all you can say is to trust my heart and listen to the mountain? That is the most cryptic non-answer there is. Listen to the mountain. Trust your heart. What is this? A fucking Disney movie? Thanks for being entirely unhelpful, Gandalf. I'm glad I wasted my time talking to you." I throw my hands in the air as I start to walk away. *Some seer he is.*

"You don't need my guidance, Walker. You already know what to do," Gandalf calls after me. Not that that's helpful either, because if I knew what to do I'd already be doing it. I wouldn't have been standing there making hooch with him for twenty minutes.

Needing to cool down, I head back to my cabin and realize that's not much help because I'm surrounded by Faith's stuff. She left in such a hurry that she packed exactly nothing. Even her laptop is still sitting on the table she was working from on Friday afternoon before we went up to the lookout. I haven't been able to bring myself to change anything about her setup. Even the mug she'd been drinking from still sits next to an open notepad with a pencil lying across the front.

The more I look at her things, the more curious and desperate for answers I become. I've never been one to pry into other people's business or to look through another's possessions. But these are extenuating circumstances.

The first thing I do is place two fingers on her notepad and drag it a little closer to me. The spiral binding has little chunks of paper caught in it, telling me a page has been torn off hastily. There are even indentations in the next sheet of paper where her cursive writing has pushed through from the previous page.

Picking up the pencil, I contemplate scribbling over the page to get the indentations to show up as writing, but something tells me to have a quick look around the cabin, and lo-and-behold I find the torn sheet of paper poking out from under the couch. I'm not sure if it fell or blew under there, but when I retrieve it, I realize hiding beneath the couch is *not* where I was supposed to find it.

Walker,

Something terrible has happened to my story, and I have to go to save it. I'm so sorry. I'll be back as soon as I've fixed the mess I've caused.

Love you always,

Faith xxx

My free hand drifts up to cover my mouth as I let out a relieved laugh. *She left a note.* It doesn't excuse her leaving me up on the mountain the way she did, but at least she left me a note and an explanation. It's the sign I so desperately needed. It tells me what I hoped was true all along—Faith never intended to embarrass the homestead like that. Something has happened along the way. And as Serena pointed out, it was probably that guy, buttmunch. *If only I could read the real article.*

That way I could take it to Brady and show him that Faith is wholeheartedly one of us. Hell, I'd take it to everyone on the homestead, make them read it, then let them know I'm going to Anchorage to get her. The mountain chose her for me, which means the mountain chose her for *us*. The homestead is where she belongs.

But without that original article, it's going to be a hard sell getting everyone to welcome her back. Unless...

Taking a seat at the table, I open her laptop and wait for it to wake up. It's asking me for a password, and I have to admit I have no fucking clue what it is. But I do know Faith. And if she's used anything important to her as her login, then I should be able to figure that out.

I try her favorite color first. Then her birthdate. Then her favorite color with the year of her birth. Then I put her pet hamster, Steve, in with the year of her birth and *boom*, I'm in. "Fuck. I'm a hacker. I think I missed my calling," I say to no one, feeling thoroughly impressed with myself. *Huxley better watch out, I'll be taking over his IT responsibilities soon enough.*

I click the mouse to open the article. That's when I find out what I felt sure of from the beginning. Faith didn't write a single bad word about the homestead. She wrote a well-thought-out article about communal living and a glowing representation of sustainability and the minimal impact a bio-diverse settlement has on the surrounding environment. And when I glance through her email chain with her boss, I feel sure that he's responsible for everything. He set her up. He set us all up. And he made us look foolish. Now, *that* is something we homesteaders don't take lightly.

Before I can even give my next decision another thought, I'm grabbing my keys and heading back outside. I see Nash as I'm driving out of the compound, but he just smiles and waves. I think he knows exactly where I'm going and why. *It's time to bring my girl back home.*

21

FAITH

Thanksgiving is usually my favorite of all the holidays, but this year it's barely registering that it's supposed to be a happy time, a time for being grateful for everything and everyone in your life. It's impossible to feel grateful when I'm just...empty. And the pain in my chest continues to grow stronger with every day that passes. It's been two weeks since I left Walker in that mountaintop cabin; two weeks since I left the mountain, driving on a mad dash to somehow fix the damage from the story Marvin published with my byline. *I failed...*

Marvin is claiming editorial discretion, even despite the retraction and my original story being published. It was a big move by Giles to do that, given our new sky-high readership numbers. But he says credibility is everything, and he won't have his paper knowingly spreading lies. Marvin is still the editor-in-chief, though. He's been issued a warning because *technically* he just offered a differing viewpoint over what's going on on the mountain. He doesn't even seem to have a shred of remorse over it, either. He really is a despicable human. And despite the paper publishing the truth in the end, the damage has already been done. Now I can't show my face on the mountain until I somehow repair it.

I've been trying to work on the series of articles I was going to write about the mountain and publish them myself instead of trusting the like of buttmunch to do right by the homestead. I want to shine a spotlight on the good people on and around the mountain to show what life is *really* like there. I've got a handful of contacts in the industry. Maybe I could create my own blog and get some of those articles syndicated to help spread the word that biodiversity works. We could even run some workshops to teach people how to do their bit at home.

The ideas are all there, but whenever I sit down to write, the words won't come out. I'd hoped to use the growing interest in the homestead to push my new agenda—to put the true story out there so that people know how wonderful the homestead and the work of the founding sons truly is. It should be championed, not condemned. They're no more a cult than any other free-thinking community, and I hate that anyone could think badly of them. I even heard there are demonstrators at the gates now. *How awful.*

The phone calls and messages from Serena and Walker have all but stopped. Serena's last message to me simply stated, *"It will all work out. Just believe in what you had and how you felt. It's the only way to get through the pain."* And I've tried—God, how I've tried—but the longer I'm away from the mountain, from Walker, the harder it is to stay strong. The past few days I've been falling deeper and deeper into a dark black hole, the light at the top getting dimmer.

"Gorgeous girl, I know you're not OK," my Mom says, perching on the edge of my bed where I've been hiding away ever since I arrived back in Kinleyville yesterday. Now it's Thanksgiving and when I'd normally be in the kitchen, helping Mom cook her signature Baked King Crab and Nigliq soup for our town's Thanksgiving potluck meal this afternoon—a tradition we've had for as long as I can remember—I'm sequestered away in my room instead, trying to pretend the hurt isn't still there.

I can't even bring myself to get dressed and face people. I just want to hide away and mourn the loss of a life I thought I'd have. I can't even see how Walker and I can come back from this. The homestead is his legacy, his history, it was supposed to be our future too, and I turned it into a laughingstock, *a cult.* I will never forgive myself for allowing this to happen. I should have *known* something was up when Marvin was cooperating. *God, I hate that man!*

He's stolen away the hope and excitement I had, planning a new life up on the mountain, spending the holidays with my fiance and bringing him down here to meet my parents, and packing up my old life for the promise of a new one. It would have been the first time I've ever introduced a man to my family, and now...none of it is happening. There's nothing to be thankful for except alcohol, because that's the only way I manage to get a moment of sleep each night.

"You did nothing wrong with that story, darling," Mom says as she strokes my hair, her eyes filled with concern as she looks down at me. "It's been two weeks now, and you're still beating yourself up about it. You didn't make that nasty editor change your words. And you've done *everything* you can to put things right. None of this nastiness was your doing. You have to know that. And I'm worried about how it's affecting you—you're not eating, I know you're not sleeping, and you're not even writing when you, my girl, are someone who *has* to write. It's your passion, your purpose. A world without your words isn't much of a world at all."

Tears fill my eyes. "But look what that *passion* has done? It's caused untold pain and anger and heartache to people who were nothing but kind, and sweet. They welcomed me into their lives with open arms, and I didn't even *consider* the position I was putting them in.

I *opened* that door Marvin used to exploit them. I have to own that. And then there's Walker...I..." I sob as his name leaves my lips. "Mom, how can I expect him to forgive me when I can't even forgive myself? If I'd never proposed the story, then none of this would ever have happened. If I'd focused on what was happening rather than losing myself in the man I love, I could've realized and stopped it before it went too far. I *hate* myself for what I've done."

"Enough," my father bellows from the doorway. "Faith Marie Johnson, you are not going to lie there and beat yourself up any longer." My spine goes straight like it did when I was a kid and Dad gave me a piece of his mine. Even at twenty-three, it still has the same effect. "We raised our daughter to be a fighter and to never give up, even when the cards are stacked against you. You don't wallow in self-pity like a quitter."

"But—"

"No buts. You're fading away in front of my eyes and I won't stand for it. You're strong, you're smart, and I *know* that the man standing downstairs in the den wouldn't have traveled all this way to ask for my permission to marry you if he wasn't a good, well-raised man. *That* man has his head screwed on straight and he knows a good thing when he sees her. And considering he just flat out told me you're the love of his life and he'd do anything for you, I think that's a man who deserves to be heard." Then my dad lifts his chin and disappears from my room while my mother and I just stare at each other.

"He's here?" I whisper, my body frozen, my eyes wide as my father's words sink in.

"I think so," Mom says, excitement coating her tone as I sit up. *Walker is here. Walker. Is. Here.*

Thump. Thump. Thump. There's no mistaking that my love, my soul mate, is nearby. My heart feels like it's been shocked back to life, the pain I've grown so used to is suddenly gone.

I jump out of bed, my Mom's soft laugh filling the room. "Careful, Faith, you don't want to injure yourself before you even get down there to see him."

"But he's here, Mom. He's here!" I smile, giddy as I scour the room for clothes to wear, finding a discarded pair of jeans on the floor and Walker's flannel shirt that I've been living in since I left, his smell comforting me on the nights we were apart.

When I'm finally dressed, Mom stands by the door, reaching out to grab my hand before I leave. "You deserve happiness, Faith. You deserve the love of a good man like I have with your father. If Walker is the love of your life, then do *not* let your self-perceived failure hold you back from the life you want...the life you've *earned* by being a good person, a *just* person, a *moral* person. Go and grab your happiness with *both* hands, my love."

I wrap my arms around her, sighing into her neck as she hugs me tight. "Thank you, mom."

"Now, go see this Walker fellow. But tell him, you're *both* expected to stay for Thanksgiving dinner at the church hall. I can lose my daughter to the mountain tomorrow, but today, we feast. OK?"

Shifting back, I meet her warm gentle eyes and for the first time since that fateful morning on the mountain top, I smile.

22

WALKER

Mr. Johnson makes his way down the stairs and I'm quick to stand up, eager to hear if I can expect Faith to come downstairs. Not that her refusal to come down and speak to me would change anything, I'd just barrel up those stairs and force my way into her room. And failing that, I'd just yell through the door until she has no choice but to listen to me. Sure, that sounds crazy. But I'm also crazy in love with her. She's the one the mountain chose for me, and even if the mountain *didn't* choose her, you can be sure as hell I'd have chosen her myself. She is the other half of my heart, the completion of my soul, and the one thing I most definitely cannot live without. The last two weeks apart have proved that without a shadow of a doubt.

"She should be down in just a moment. Seems rather pleased to know you're here," Mr. Johnson says with a smirk. He's an older man, slight in stature with a pleasant disposition. When I showed up here earlier, he was more than happy to listen to my plea even though I was more than happy to *beg* for an audience. We sat down amicably, and I explained that I knew Faith didn't write that article. I told him I didn't blame her for a second for the things her boss said about us. I also explained that I was enamored with his daughter, and I wouldn't be leaving without her. "I plan to marry her, sir," I said, keeping my eyes locked with his. "And I'd appreciate your blessing on that."

Mr. Johnson leaned forward and steepled his fingers together. "You're asking a lot for a man I only learned about when my daughter turned up on our doorstep sobbing with a big diamond on her finger," he said, eyeing me carefully. "But I'm also aware that you aren't the reason behind those tears. She loves you, and for that reason alone, I'll go upstairs and talk her into coming down to hear you out. But my blessing...that will come after I see my daughter smiling again."

"Then I'll take that as a yes, sir. I'm the man who makes your daughter happy."

"We'll see about that," he said before going upstairs. It wasn't difficult to overhear the bellowing from where I sat waiting in the den, and I have to say it made me smile. He gave her a stern talking to, but all of his words were said with care as he reminded her of the strong, capable, *loved* woman she is. And now, all I can hear from upstairs is rushed footsteps and excited voices.

“I think you’re about to get that smile, sir,” I tell Mr. Johnson as I step toward the stairs and watch as Faith’s toes come into view. They’re painted red, and they’re as perfect as the rest of her.

“In that case, my blessing is yours,” he says with a chuckle as we watch Faith rushing halfway down the stairs before slowing down like she suddenly decided to act cool.

“Sweetheart,” I say, grinning from ear to ear as her beautiful face appears and our eyes lock. “I missed you.”

“Me too,” she gasps, speeding up again before she launches herself off the bottom step directly into my arms.

I catch her and spin her around, laughing as I kiss her while she cries and apologizes with so many words I can’t make them out.

“None of it matters, my love. The article, the public reaction, the demonstrators at the homestead...none of it...it doesn’t matter. The world will move on soon enough, and at most we’ll be a punchline or better yet, completely forgotten, some distant memory lining the bottom of bird cages.”

"But it was my fault. I'm the one who caused it all. If I hadn't been trying to have my cake and eat it too, the homestead wouldn't be under the microscope like it is. I honestly thought I was helping raise awareness, but all I did was cause a scandal. And I tried, Walker, I tried to get them to stop it. But I was too late. Marvin made a fool out of me, he demonized all of you, and I'm just...I'm so incredibly sorry." Her smile is shaky as her voice cracks and her eyes glisten with unshed tears. *My gorgeous girl has been beating herself up about this.*

"Want to know what I'm sorry about?" I ask as I lower her to the ground and brush my fingers through her silky hair while she nods. "I'm sorry that you felt like you couldn't talk to us about this. That you felt you had to run away and *stay* away because you couldn't fix it. I wish you'd trusted in the mountain, more importantly, I wish you'd trusted in *us*. There is nothing in this world you could ever do that would make me stop loving you. The last thing I ever wanted was distance or time away. Your place is right here"—I slide my hands down her arms and entwine our fingers—"with me. Wherever you go, I go. Wherever I go, you go. We belong, Faith. And you have to have *actual* faith in our connection that I'm sure you feel in your heart."

"I do," she whispers. "I feel it. And my god it hurts when I'm not with you."

“Then why didn't you come *home*?” I whisper, releasing her hands and pulling her closer, my arm sliding around her waist as I cup her cheek, wiping away her tears with my thumb. “You had to know I was in pain without you, too.”

“I did. I just... I didn't feel I deserved you. What I did. What my actions caused... It makes me feel sick that anyone could think that about the homestead. I thought if I came back before I fixed everything... I was afraid you wouldn't want me anymore.” Her face crumples and the tears fall freely down her face. I wipe away as many as I can but ultimately lose the battle. The only thing I can do is kiss her deep and slow to show her how intense my feelings still are.

By the time we come up for air, her tears have stopped, and she’s completely breathless. This is when I realize her parents are still there watching our reunion, her mother is even fanning her face.

“Oh my,” she says, nodding as she looks between me and Faith. “If you don’t marry him, darling, I just might have to take him off your hands.”

Mr. Johnson clears his throat. “I believe you’re already spoken for, May.”

“Yes. But you don’t kiss me like *that,*” she says, which prompts Mr. Johnson to wrap his arms around her middle and kiss the life out of her, tilting her backward until one of her legs lifts for balance.

Faith giggles as she watches the display, and I grin just because I'm holding her again. When Mr. Johnson releases his wife, she pats her hair, a deep blush coloring her cheeks. "Well, I think we've all got a *lot* to be thankful for this year." Her eyes move to me. "I don't believe we've officially met. I'm May, Faith's mom." She holds out her hand and I take it before pressing a kiss to her knuckles.

"Walker Long. It's a pleasure to meet you, ma'am."

As May steps back, Mr. Johnson steps forward and shakes my hand, beaming as he takes in his daughter's smiling face. "Welcome to the family, son. The name's Bernie. First names only from now on."

"Unless you want to call us Mom and Dad," May blurts. "That's also fine with us. I'm so pleased to welcome you into the Johnson clan. We hear you have a big mountain family. We're both very eager to visit sometime soon."

"You're more than welcome. I was thinking about a New Year's Eve wedding," I say, glancing down at Faith to see what she thinks. "How does that sound for everyone?"

"So soon?" May asks. "That's just wonderful. I can't wait. Bernie, we're going to Bear Mountain for the new year!"

"So I hear," he says, still beaming happily. "But first, I think we should be getting to the potluck in town. I can't wait to announce your engagement. There'll be a few ranchers there who are disappointed another eligible Kinleyville bachelorette is being spirited away to the mountain."

"We all have to go to where our heart calls," Faith says as she leans into me. "And my heart only wants you, Walker."

"Then I guess we'd better go and tell the townsfolk you're spoken for," I say.

"And eat!" May says. "I'm starved."

"So am I," Faith says. "I feel like I haven't eaten in forever."

"That's because you haven't," Bernie mutters as we all clamor toward the door, putting coats on and piling in the one car, food in laps as we drive to the church hall. Then we spend the rest of the day feasting and being thankful.

"I love you so much, Walker," Faith whispers as she rests her head on my shoulder.

"I love you too, sweetheart," I say, pressing a kiss to the top of her head and inhaling deeply. Tomorrow we'll go to Anchorage and pack up her apartment, ready to start our life together on the mountain. Soon I'll have the woman I love back with me at the homestead where she belongs. My heart has been restored. Tomorrow can't come soon enough.

23

FAITH

Walker is taping up the final box of my belongings in the living room when I walk into the room. He looks up and grins at me, the smile reaching his eyes and transforming his entire face. He looks happy, *really* happy, and I love knowing I'm the reason.

"Did you sort things out with your landlord?"

I nod. "Yeah. I'm good to leave whenever. I just have to organize a cleaner and drop the keys off.

"You got a neighbor?"

"Yeah. Mrs. Augustino next door. I used to go there and have Sunday dinner with her every week whenever I could. She kind of adopted Serena and I when we first moved in here. We were like stand-in grandchildren since hers live down south."

Walker's gaze softens. "Would she be OK with helping you out with this?"

"For sure." I don't know why, but my throat tightens and tears well in my eyes. Walker stands and moves to comfort me, wrapping his arms around my back and pulling me in close.

"Sweetheart. I know this is moving really fast. Are you OK?" he murmurs as I bury my face in his chest.

I nod and shore myself up, letting the warmth of Walker's hug seem into me. This feels so damn right, and Walker needs to know just how on board I am with this move, and with him. I lift my head and look up at my beautiful mountain man who I can't wait to start my life with.

I cup his jaw in my hands, ensuring I have his full attention. "I've never been more sure about anything in my entire life. You're my future. My first and last love, and I'm never going to be anywhere but by your side." His lips curve up as I drop my voice to a sultry whisper. "And if the bed wasn't dismantled right now, I'd be *showing* you just how certain I am that you are, hands down, the *best* thing to ever happen to me."

Walker's head turns, his eyes scanning the almost empty room. "I can get creative if you can?"

And that's how our packing gets waylaid for a while as we make use of the living room wall, and then my shower one last time before we go.

With the call of our body's taken care of, we finish packing Walker's truck to the brim with my stuff. Anything I'm not taking today will be donated to charity since I don't need it anymore.

"You ready to start a new adventure with me, sweet-heart?" Walker fires up the engine and reaches out to tangle our fingers, tilting his gaze to meet mine.

"I can't wait." I lift his knuckles and brush my lips against his skin, earning a rumble deep inside his chest. "But I just need to make one more stop before we head home. Is that OK?"

"Anything you want. Tell me where to go and I'll take you there." I give him directions and his brows go up, but then his smile becomes so bright I swear it could blind me, pride and approval shining in his eyes. "Fuck, yes," he growls as he parks the truck then hooks his hand behind my neck, tugging me in for a hard, hot, fast kiss.

Fifteen minutes later, I'm strolling into the offices of the Anchorage Press, a white envelope in my hand and determination steeling my spine.

"Hey, Faith," Grant calls out as soon as he sees me.

"Hey, Grant. Have you still got my box of stuff packed up?" I ask.

"Sure do, lady. Here you go. But first a hug." I stop in front of his desk and hug him, a silent thank you for being my eyes and ears during the past few hectic and painful weeks.

"Thank you. For everything."

He shrugs and shoots me a grin. "I'm an old softie deep down. You've found your soulmate and you're starting a whole new life with him on the homestead that is *not* a cult. Just do me one thing, OK?"

"Yeah, sure. Anything..."

"Send me an invite to the wedding," he says with a wink, making me laugh.

"Now *that* I can do." I pick up my box of belongings from Grant, and with a wave to the rest of my colleagues, I walk with purpose to Marvin's office, strolling in without bothering to knock.

His head jerks back when his eyes twist to mine. "Faith. I didn't expect you in the office today." His gaze drops to the box in my hand. "Going somewhere?" he asks, arching a brow. I step forward and place my letter of resignation on his desk, the anger that has been swirling inside of me since I first read his hack of a story about the homestead building to a crescendo now.

"You are the most arrogant, egotistical, narcissistic piece of baloney I have ever met and worked for. You took what was one of my best articles and twisted it into an uneducated, untrue, and slanderous exposé that caused disruption, shame, and embarrassment to people I now call family. You are a disgrace to journalism and I *know* you'll get what's coming to you, whether that be tomorrow, next week, or in the future."

"Is that a threat?"

"Oh no, buttmunch. That's a damn guarantee. So if you don't know this already, I quit! And good riddance to you." Then I lift my head up high and strut out of there to slow claps, which gradually turn into a round of applause. And that, ladies and gentlemen, is how I got my own back. It wasn't some huge big showdown with buttmunch, but it gave me the closure I needed to drive off into the sunset with my husband-to-be by my side, headed toward my new home. Destination: Bear Mountain Homestead.

Walker must've called ahead because when we drive through the gates and come to stop in front of The Den, everyone is there waiting for us—all the founding as well as Serena, Martie, Van, their one-year-old daughter Vera, Patty and Rick, and of course, Gandalf.

My chest feels lighter yet tight at the same time. "Are you sure they don't hate me?" I whisper. As quick as a flash, my seatbelt is undone and Walker hauls me over to sit in his lap, his hands cradling my jaw like I'm the most precious thing in the world to him—just as he is to me.

"Sweetheart, everyone knows you and knows your heart, there is no anger or animosity here, Brady and I wouldn't allow it, anyway. This is a welcoming committee, and it's all for *you*. They want you here almost as much as I do."

"God, I love you, Walker Long."

"Love you more, Faith Marie Johnson."

I bury my face in his neck as he hugs me to him.

"I have one more thing to ask you..." I whisper in his ear, squirming in his lap against his growing hardness.

"What's that?"

"Can we, um.... greet the welcoming committee *after* going to our cabin."

"Fuck yeah we can," he growls, groaning as he lifts me off his lap to sit right by his side. He pulls the truck up beside the group and winds down the window. "Gonna have to take a raincheck on this reunion. Faith has other plans." He turns to Nash. "And bud, just a word of warning, you're up next, so you better open your eyes and look out for your One. Because she's coming, and if it's anything like what Brady and I went through, you're gonna need all the help you can get."

Then he revs the engine and takes me to our cabin, proceeding to carry me over the threshold and keeping me *busy* for the rest of the night.

And I wouldn't have wanted it any other way.

EPILOGUE 1

FAITH

Five years later...

"Hey, River," I say, walking into the offices of the Kenshaw Gazette.

"Hey, *boss*," River replies with a smirk.

After moving to the mountain with Walker, I took a break to just enjoy living at the homestead and reconnecting with all the residents, mending bridges, even though Walker told me it wasn't needed. But it felt necessary. Even though I knew I was simply a pawn in buttmunch's game, I still felt responsible. However, my guilt quickly evaporated when I was welcomed back into the fold with wide-open arms.

I also set out to do what I promised to myself—write and publish a series of blog posts about life on the mountain, in the homestead, and the wonderful people living here. Just like the scandal piece that had me running away after Walker's proposal, my blog went viral and five years later, it's still going strong with continually growing daily visitors and amazing engagement from readers. It's now morphed into more of a sustainable living information source. We highlight different gardening, composting, eco-friendly practices, and our experiences/successes/failures here at the homestead.

That's when I called River, the then editor of the local paper, and asked if the job offer was still available. It was, and I've spent the last five years writing features and human interest pieces about people around the district and helping grow the paper into what it is today—a bigger publication with a state-wide readership. Another development was River stepping down and handing me the reins.

He still works here, but we instigated a role swap. Now he's the one picking and choosing stories, and I run the paper. We've moved to mostly working remotely, which enables us to keep our footprint small but our reach large, with reporters all over the state to serve our readers better. It also lets me stay home in our massive expanded cabin with our two girls, Ava, four, and Monroe, one.

"Why are you sitting there like we *don't* have an issue going live tomorrow?" I ask, quirking a brow as I lean against the doorway to River's office.

"Because it's all done and dusted, it's just waiting for our lovely *editor* to press publish."

"Oh," I say, suddenly confused. "Then why the hell are you here?"

He chuckles and shakes his head. "I could ask you the same thing, mama to be," he says, nodding to my six-month baby bump.

I rub my hand over my stomach and grin. "I came to check up on *you*."

"I call bullshit."

Sighing, I move into the office and sit down on the sofa next to the desk. "Walker has taken the girls fishing."

"Your husband took a three-year-old and one-year-old *fishing*?"

"Yeah. And if I stay home, I'm just going to pace back and forth waiting for them to come home."

"*Or* you could sit down, put your feet up, and enjoy the silence of an empty cabin, since soon enough, you're not going to have many quiet moments."

"But the paper—"

"Can wait. It's all done, and you can—and should—be delegating so that you *can* take these moments to sit back, relax, and *not* think about anything except growing that mini-Long of yours."

Said baby kicks my bladder as if agreeing with the man.

"OK. Jeez. You know you sound just like my husband, right?"

River smirks. "Walker is a smart man."

I smile at just the thought of my doting, loyal, hard-working husband who goes to mush as soon as he walks through the door and sees his girls. Walker has made sure that I've never regretted moving to the mountain—just as I've never stopped working hard to make right the wrongs that almost cost me this life five years ago.

"Right. I'm making an executive, former editor-in-chief decision so that you can get your butt home and enjoy the mountain serenity before chaos returns." River turns back to his computer and brings up the paper's website, and with a challenging brow lift my way, he clicks submit and just like that, the latest edition of the Kenshaw Gazette is live and out there in the world. Our print edition will go out around the district tomorrow, which means I *can* take the rest of the day off.

"Well then, I guess we both need to get out of here," I say, pushing up off the arm of the sofa and back to my feet. "Ugh," I grunt as the baby kicks me again.

"What? Are you OK?" River says, his eyes wide with panic.

I giggle and shake my head at him. "Yeah, my child just thinks my stomach is a trampoline he—or she—needs to jump, kick, and punch on."

River's gaze twinkles with amusement. "Ah yes. Well, you *are* the one who decided to have *three* children."

My lips curve up into a content smile. "No. The *mountain* spirit blessed me with three children. Maybe more if Walker has his way. But I love it." I cradle my bump. "Life is good, Riv. I've never been happier. The best thing I ever did was drive Bertha to the homestead for Serena's wedding."

"No, the best thing you ever did was say yes to marrying me," Walker's low husky voice says from the doorway.

I gasp and spin around. "What are you doing here? More importantly, *where* are our girls?"

He pushes off the frame and crosses the room. "I'm here to get my workaholic wife to leave the office, and our girls are having a playdate with Aunt Rena and Uncle Brady and their cousins."

"Oh," I say.

"Hey, River. Mind if I kidnap my wife?" Walker asks. River's lips twitch.

"I was just telling her to go home and relax." He stands and looks between Walker and I. "See ya next week,

Faith," he muses, knowing I'm about to be frog-marched out of here by my protective husband.

Watching River's retreating back, I turn back to my husband's narrowed eyes. He's forever telling me I need more work/life balance—more working around life instead of living around work.

"I was just—"

"Not delegating."

"But—"

Walker rests his index finger to my lips, silencing me. "Sweetheart, we have the whole afternoon to ourselves with no squeals, crying, screeching, or True and the Rainbow Kingdom on repeat. Do you wanna stand here being cute and arguing with me over your inherent need to work, *or*..."

"Take me home and help me relax, baby," I say seductively, leaning in close to my husband and touching the tip of my tongue to his finger on my lips.

"With fucking pleasure," he rasps before wrapping his arms around my back and slamming his lips down on mine.

For the record, my husband took me home, wound me up then *relaxed* me a few times that afternoon before we walked out of our cabin hand in hand to get our girls back.

EPILOGUE 2

WALKER

Ten years later...

"If you could have anything for Christmas this year, what would it be?" Faith asks as she stands over me. I'm lying in bed, ready for some shut eye after a long day, and she's standing directly over me, bouncing on the mattress in her underwear because *somehow* she still has energy. Not that I'm complaining. The view is spectacular.

"I literally want for nothing," I say, grinning. "I have everything I'll ever need. Four beautiful daughters, a gorgeous wife, and my life on the mountain. I'd say I'm pretty complete."

"You wouldn't want, say...a son?" she asks as she stops bouncing and drops to her knees before she straddles on top of me.

"Why would you ask that?" I narrow one eye and keep my tone cautious as I slide my palms along the smooth skin of her thighs.

"Well...I was reading an article about conception, and it seems that if we hold off until the day I ovulate, then we're more likely to get a boy." She shifts slightly on my lap, my growing arousal pressing between her legs.

"You think we can hold off, do you? Sweetheart, we barely go a full twelve hours without tearing each other's clothes off."

"I know." She bites her lip as she runs her fingernails through my chest hair. "But it'll be fun trying, don't you think? I'd love a little boy running around here. Walker Junior has a nice ring to it, don't you think?"

"I do. But I also think that what you're proposing sounds like pure torture. How do we even know when you're ovulating?"

"I pee on a stick, monitor my temperature, spit on a magnifying thingy."

"That all sounds super exciting. But seriously, babe, I love you and I love my girls. We don't need to do anything special to try to game the system into giving us a boy. If the mountain wanted boys for us, we'd have them."

"But I want to try," she pouts, giving a look that just melts me.

"Fine," I say, entwining my fingers with hers. "I'll keep my dick loaded until your pee or spit or whatever says it's time to unload."

"You say the most romantic things, Walker Long," she says with a giggle as she slides off me, leaving me aching for her as she snuggles in beside me. "Good night, baby. I love you."

"I love you too," I say, bringing her closer as I stare up at the ceiling, keyed up and regretting this waiting game with every moment that passes.

But eventually, I manage to get some sleep. And thankfully, it isn't long before she's calling me back to the cabin for the 'unloading ceremony', as I've been calling it. Even Nash is glad when I get the call. He said he thought Brady was the only one of us capable of walking around acting like a bear with a toothache, but I'd managed to top that with my daily grumblings.

In the end, it turns out perfectly though. Exactly three days before Christmas, Faith and I are at the obstetrician's office getting an ultrasound when we receive the good news. Baby number five is a boy for Faith and Walker Long. Faith cries happy tears, and I have to admit I have a bit of a weep too. I meant it when I said I was happy with my girls, but I feel blessed to have a little boy to add to our brood as well. Looks like I'll need to add another bedroom to our cabin. Bear Mountain Homestead seems to be growing exponentially with all the Homestead brother's finding their

Ones and having kids. Pretty soon, we'll have to stop letting new people in. Or better yet, maybe we'll just expand and build our own school, bring our children up with the land and teach them how to apply learned skills to our way of life. It could be a beautiful thing. We could even get Nash's girl to paint murals in all the classrooms. She's a gun with a brush and an idea, and she certainly likes to keep Nash on his toes. But that's a story for another day, I suppose. For now, I'll just focus on the fact that my wife is growing my first son in her belly, truly making me the happiest man in all the mountains.

Before Faith came to the homestead, I felt like I was constantly trying to prove myself and fill another man's shoes. But she taught me that the man I am is more than enough for everyone. Sometimes the internal voice in our head is harder on us than everyone else is, and it takes someone kind enough to really see you to make you see your true worth. Through her series of articles about the mountain and our eco-friendly, communal living, Faith showed me that I'd long been the leader I always strived to be.

Now, years later, I'm still a leader. But I like to share that role with my homestead brothers. We all have families and little ones these days, so we have a roster that gives us time off with our families, while making sure the homestead runs seamlessly. I don't think we've ever felt more content and plentiful. Having children around means we get to continue our legacy for generations to come. Sure, there might be a time when they leave the mountain and attempt to do other things. But as sure as it called to all of us, the mountain will bring them back, right where they belong, so the future generations will continue to thrive under the mountain's watchful eye. And you never know, one day, Gandalf might come out with a prophecy about another mountain.

I hear the ranchers who took over Serena's dad's supply store are from Eagle Mountain. I would not be surprised if there's a new mother to continue the call over there, eventually. But who it might be. A Cooper? A Homesteader? Only time—and Gandalf's magic book—will tell.

Until then, I'll be sitting pretty with my gorgeous wife by my side, and the mountain in my heart because life is good, and the future, it's even better.

The End

well...only if you stop reading...

Up next is our grumpiest Long brother, Nash, and an artist who's new in town. You can read Nash's story in Artist Seeks Mountain Man.

And I have a special treat for you Mountaineers! Christmas is coming up and I've put together a holiday story, Moose Mountain style! You'll get to revisit all of your favorite couples and find out how they're spending their Christmas together in Mountain Seeking Santa

SIGN up for my newsletter to receive release day emails: https://www.subscribepage.com/marleymichaels

Don't forget to add marleymichaelswrites@gmail.com to your address book!

If you're on social media, you can catch me on Facebook

https://www.facebook.com/authormarleymichaels/

or join my reader group

www.facebook.com/groups/856031968231022

Or you can follow me on Instagram

https://instagram.com/marleymichaelswrites

Can't wait to have more fun on the Mountains with you!

MORE BY MARLEY MICHAELS

Moose Mountain Brothers

Author Seeking Mountain Man

Introvert Seeking Mountain Man

Fangirl Seeking Mountain Man

Hiker Seeking Mountain Man

Men of Moose Mountain

Mountain Seeking Doctor

Mountain Seeking Pilot

Mountain Seeking Hero

Mountain Seeking Fire Chief

Mountain Seeking Veterinarian

Mountain Seeking Princess

Mountain Seeking Santa

Bear Mountain Brothers

Wallflower Seeks Mountain Man

Reporter Seeks Mountain Man

Artist Seeks Mountain Man

Printed in Great Britain
by Amazon

75541858R00132